Secret Peace Corp
Planet Ares
Driftwood Eagle

Secret Peace Corp

Planet Ares

Driftwood Eagle

BOOK THREE OF THIS SERIES

John Jones

Library of Congress Control Number:		2019901009
ISBN:	Hardcover	978-1-7960-1257-6
	Softcover	978-1-7960-1256-9
	eBook	978-1-7960-1255-2

This is a work of fiction. All of the characters, names, incidents, organizations, and dialogue in this novel are either the products of the author's imagination or are used fictitiously.

Note: THIS BOOK CONTAINS ADULT LANGUAGE.

For information related to the Front Cover, see Foot Note 1.

Print information available on the last page.

Rev. date: 01/28/2019

To order additional copies of this book, contact:
Xlibris
1-888-795-4274
www.Xlibris.com
Orders@Xlibris.com
791538

Contents

Preface

This Series of Books will continue to introduce man in person with his maker God Almighty. God will meet and work with Representatives from the Planet Ares (PA) to seek help in finding "Peace" Throughout His Entire Universe. God uses these meetings as a method to allow man to seek "Peace on his own terms".

The Primary Setting for this continuing Secret Peace Corp Story is located in the United States of America (U.S.A.) in the State of Virginia on the Eastern Shore.

Secret Peace Corp (SPC) Agent John James VA10A and his wife Susan James SPC Agent VA10C have been assigned a SPC Mission by their Commanding Officer Joshua Christian (JC) from the Secret Peace Corp Earth Base Station (SPCEBS).

This SPC Mission is to seek out, locate and verify if a small al-Qaida Terrorist Cell located on the Delmarva Peninsula exists and is expanding.

SPC Agents VA10A and VA10C investigate and locate this Cell Code name "The Delly Rode". During their investigation they are shocked and surprised to discover that this "Delly Rode Cell" is in the process of planning two major missions at this time. One; is to Hijack an EXOSET MISSILE Code name "DRIFTWOOD EAGLE". Two; is to construct, plant and detonate a High Yield Dynamite Bomb within the Wallops Island Space Center Complex (WISC) Wallops Island, Virginia.

How the Mysteries of these two Missions develop and unfold will surely overwhelm your mind as this Story is told.

These Two Missions come together as the SPC continues to seek "Peace Here on Planet Earth" (PE).

Dedications

To my wife LaVerne (Susie) among many family and friends that have kept me inspired to continue this Series of Books my third effort at writing. Of course I still do not want to leave out all those that laughed.

Sentiments

I believe in GOD, don't you? Hell I am not perfect. All I can do is ask for Forgiveness!!!!

Chapter 1

INTRODUCTION

This Series continues, as the Secret Peace Corp (SPC) from Planet Ares (PA) continues to Promote "Peace" here on Planet Earth (PE).

To fully understand the SPC and its reasons to seek out PE and establish a Base Station here and the use of their advanced SPC Weapons it is Highly Recommended that the Reader first read Book One of this Series; "Secret Peace Corp Planet Ares". International Standard Book Number (ISBN), ISBN 978-1-5434-3531-3.

Book Two is also recommended for reading pleasure and to follow this continuing Series.

"Secret Peace Corp Planet Ares Wood Duck Ridge" ISBN 978-1-9845-3477-4!

The Primary setting for this continuing Story is located in the United States of America (U.S.A.) in the State of Virginia on the Eastern Shore. The Eastern Shore is called by many as the Delmarva Peninsula as it is the East Coast Route (Rt 13) up from the state of Virginia through the states of Maryland and Delaware. As the Ole Timey Eastern Shore Folks will tell you "Take the Ole Delly Rode", (a.k.a. Virginia State Route 13).

Chapter 2

THE RAOUL'S

This story continues on Thursday November 01, 2007. Another typical work day as Allen Raoul up early sits at his desk in his study on his beautiful Cedar View farm watching the sun gleaming off the waters of Nandua Creek!

Allen Rasoul bought this farm about ten years ago from the original Exmore family estate and named it "Cedar View Farm" The farm is approximately one hundred square acres in size and is now over grown with beautiful pine and cedar trees.

Allen Rasoul is the youngest of the three Rasoul family boys. Abraham Rasoul is the oldest. Then comes Adam followed by one kid sister Dayzee.

All of these folks were born in Afghanistan and migrated to the U.S.A. with their parents to escape the Clannish and Terrorist Wars that are destroying their Country even to this day.

The family settled in Annapolis, Maryland in a typical hard working blue collar class neighborhood. All four kids through hard work achieved excellent educations.

The entire family is devout Muslims. Unlike their parents the kids have drifted away from the peaceful side of the religion and have turned to hateful ways blaming the Christians and Jews for causing many of the problems in their home country of Afghanistan. Non-believers of their cause are INFIDELS.

All four of the Rasoul kids now fully support the al-Qaida cause to eliminate all infidels and are now members and terrorist agents.

Adam, Allen and Dayzee through Local and National news broadcasts realize that brother Abraham may have been lost in the November 09th Earthquake that destroyed his Terrorist Cell "The Rock" located in the Wood Duck Ridge (WDR) area of Afghanistan. No word from him since pretty much confirms this.

Adam as Allen and Dayzee now know had his two assigned Missions "The Newport Ship & Dock Company" and The Defense Destroyer Guided Missile DDG-911 both fail. They also know Adam is considered by local Law Enforcement Agencies a Terrorist and is being sort after as a person of extreme interest. Adam of course was able and lucky enough to escape from over in Toppers Air Field in Middlesex County late last night and drove over to Allen's Cedar View farm to find a safe haven.

Dayzee is married to a local "Born Here" man named Drew Duzz also known as (a.k.a.) "Dewey". Dewey and Dayzee own and operate a large Junk Yard Dealership and located next door to the junkyard a used car dealership. Dewey manages the junk yard, Dayzee manages the used cars. They are pillars in the community and well thought of by all.

Allen Rasoul is considered the family genius. He owns and operates a Marine Biology Academy that borders the Dewey Junk Yard. Family, close friends and most of his students sometime call him "Doc". Allen has a Doctors Degree (PHD) in Marine Biology and his knowledge of the Subject is World Renowned. His Academy Marine graduate students are highly spoken for and sort after.

Allen through hard work and help from family and friends was able to purchase the old abandon Accomac County Elementary School Building about fifteen years ago. He restored the building and reopened it as the "Allen Rasoul. Marine Academy" (ARMA). It is now a fully accredited College whose Marine Biology students are highly rated and considered some of the most outstanding Marine Biology Scientists in the World.

Chapter 3

WHAT HAPPENED

Good morning my dear brother did you sleep well? Yes Allen I sure did. Allen this is a beautiful place you have here I cannot wait to see your complete farm and your entire operation and take your twenty five cent tour HA! HA!

Are you hungry? Yes I am staved and I could eat a horse. Let's go over to the Dormitory Dining Area located in the original Exmore Family restored Barn. I called the folks still on duty and they are expecting us.

As they walk over Adam cannot believe his eyes the grounds are beautiful and everything is so well maintained. Allen why do you have part of your barn area fenced in gated and locked? We can talk about that later but first I want to know from you in detail what the hell happened?

Why did your two Missions fail? The time, the planning the cost! The loss of those suicide (Martyrdom) pilots and planes all for nothing!

Adam looks around as they begin to eat breakfast and says "is it all right if we speak here?" Yes, just keep it on a low key. The young people eating and working here are students in the ARMA not al-Qaida agents.

Adam begins to tell Allen what he thinks may have caused his two Missions to fail. The more he speaks the more upset he gets. He gets so enraged he cries out loud and bangs his fist on the table. Allen tells him to calm down as he is being heard and is disturbing other folks still in the dining area. Adam calms down holds his head in his hands and begins to weep. Allah please forgive me I failed you.

Adam looks at Allen and declares it had to be that Toppers Airport Field Manager Jim Turner and that fuckin whore Amy he shacks up with. They must have seen something on one of their snooping around trips that looked suspicious enough and contacted the local Middlesex County Sheriff Jim Wright.

Sheriff Wright must have put it all together. Allen, Sheriff Wright must have sent up controlled drones and shot down our attack planes. Somehow, some way, someone took out our planes. It had to be him as my inside people at the time were all loyal soldiers and pilots.

Allen when I get a few days rest and can set up some plans I will if you will agree, go over and take those two pieces of shit (POS) Amy and Jim out. Adam I agree with you we will eliminate them and others. All of them are nothing but low life infidel POS.

Adam we can set it up in the future but like mother use to tell us vengeance can reverse itself.

Remember always check the pool for water before you dive off the diving board or you will bust your ass. For now dear brother finish eating your breakfast and I will show you around my beautiful farm. You are going to be very surprised as we have quite an operation set up here at the Farm.

Allen before we start your tour, what do you want me to do with my old 1941 "Black Mariah" Packard Hearse I drove over in last night? Just leave it parked inside the fenced in barn parking area for now. Just do not drive it anywhere. It will be OK as long as it stays behind this locked in fenced area.

Adam let's get started we have a lot of ground to cover plus I have things up at the ARMA school I need to take care of and I know you are anxious to see your sister and meet her husband Dewey for the first time.

Chapter 4

CEDAR VIEW FARM

Adam we just as well start here at the barn since we came over for breakfast. I bought this farm about ten years ago as a personal private home but later decided to convert the entire grounds into an extension of my ARMA School.

This Barn is a small dormitory that consists of twenty four small two bedroom apartments on the two upper levels. Each level has two full washrooms / bathrooms. The women's is located at one end and the men's at the other. Both are complete with washer and drying machines.

Down on the ground floor level at one end is a kitchen, dining area and a complete Library with the latest Computer Process Units (CPU). Next to the Library is a state of the art Marine Biology Laboratory. At the other end of the ground floor level we have a large fenced in storage area plus a private meeting room I call the Squadron Ready Room (SRR).

Allen walks over to a locked door. As he unlocks the door he looks around as they step through. He closes the door quickly behind them. Adam looks at him with a straight face and says "what the hell was that all about." Just precautions, Adam you can never be too safe. Adam most of the time we have at least twenty plus students from the ARMA that work and study here. Other times we have students from other schools that visit and study here. Adam what is stored and what goes on behind these locked doors and the fenced in area is off limits to them and they are not a party to any of it. Same applies to the parking area housing your 1941 Packard Hearse. Adam I keep my School Activities and our al-Qaida Cell Activities completely separated at all times. DO YOU UNDERSTAND THAT? Yes my dear brother!!!!!!!!

As you can see this room is a typical storage room containing all our supplies necessary to support the dorm and lab etc? As they continue the tour Allan unlocks another door and again as they pass through locks it behind them. When he turns on the overhead lights Adam jumps back and cannot believe his eyes. He is completely surrounded by an arsenal of various weapons and a magazine of ammunition, hand grenades, pistols, automatic rifles you name it. Allen how in the world did you find and acquire all these weapons and this ordnance? Most of it comes from the federal U.S. government either stolen or hijacked from local Military Bases.

Adam our main problem is no High Yield explosive type ordnance. That is what we need to run a hard core al-Qaida Terrorist Cell Operation. Guns and bullets will not get the job done any more you know that. At the present time I am working on a mission I will discuss with you as ordered by Rahism Badhdadi. I am sure it must have been one of his last orders before he was killed when The Rock Cell was destroyed by the WDR Earthquake.

Adam the only High Yield ordnance that I really have in this room that I could use more of sits over here. Five cases of high yield dynamite round sticks and a box of detonating caps with pulsating wires. Adam walks over and checks out the cases of dynamite. Allen you son of a bitch (SOB)! So it was you that bought the other five cases. I tried to buy those from that ass hole (AH) Paiman up at Short Pump and he said "they were already sold and spoken for." Hell I was going to buy them for you and you beat me to it. All ten stolen cases of dynamite came from the Conyers Loft Mountain Construction Site. Allen you got five cases and I got five cases. My dear brother great minds work together that's for sure HA! HA!

Allen speaking of Dynamite and Weapons; I have one case of dynamite left sitting in that casket inside the 1941 Packard Hearse plus a few rifles, pistols and a money cube (MC) containing about $200K can I bring all that material in here? You do! Yes by all means Adam bring it all in here and store it, I need that fuckin money bad as I am broke and running this operation on a damn shoe string.

Allen clicks on his Cell Phone (CPH). Hess this is Allen contact Baka and you two meet me in the barn storage area pretty damn quick (PDQ). Yes sir we are working close by we will be there in a second. When they arrive Allen introduces his brother Adam to Hess and Baka. Hess is my Main Supervisor and Baka is his Assistant. They both live full time on site in the main house on the second floor. Hess runs this place like a Swiss Watch. Do not fuck with him and don't piss him off as they all laugh. Guy's, Adam will be staying with us for a while; he drove in late last night. Yes I know I had to get up late last night and unlock the front gate so the AH could get in HA! HA! Sorry about that.

Hess here is what I want you guys to do; take Adam's Packard Hearse keys unlock the back door and bring all the contents packed in the casket in here for storage except the MC. Take the MC up to my third floor apartment in the Main House and lock it in my study storage closet for now. Got you covered Doc. As they leave they both tell Adam "nice to have you onboard if you need anything just give us a "holler". Thank you fellows! Two great hard working folks loyal to the cause!

Adam let's get going now and head on up to the ARMA school building. I want you to see the school and then go over to see your sister and meet your brother in-law for the first time, "Dewey". You are going to shit when you meet him he is a trip, born and raised right here on the "Shore". By the way if you are not born here you are known as a "Come Here" it's an old fashion tradition, beats me, I do not know why, do not ask!!!!

Allen's CPH rings, yes Hess what is it? Doc everything in the 1941 Packard Hearse checks out OK but the MC. The MC is just an empty box. Adam this is Hess he is telling me your MC is just an empty box. Bull Shit (BS) when I packed it at Toppers Air Field early last week it had about $200K in it. Well its empty now! Damn Adam what do you supposed happened to all those U. S. Benny's inside that MC box. Beats the shit out of me the only person that could get in and out of that Hangar "A" building while we were all gone is the Topper's Air field manager Jim Turner. Adam that SOB is your man. Allen when I get a chance I will drive over and take care of that SOB you can bet your sweet ass on that. Well it's nothing we can do about it now let's head on up to the ARMA School House. Thanks Hess just store the other items we will take care of the MC problem later.

Hess we are leaving now to go up to the ARMA School House if you need me I will be there or over at Dewey's junk yard front office.

Chapter 5

DEWEY & DAYZEE DUZZ

As Allen and Adam leave the Cedar View Farm they drive down the long winding lane to the Electronic and highly alarmed steel front gate. Adam if you ever see this gate left open for any reason call me, Hess or Baka. When you drive through make sure you close it behind you and it clearly locks. You got that!!! Yes Sir Allen!!!

Allen heads on out and turns north on Route (Rt) 13, a.k.a. as the "Ole Delly Rode" towards New Church and Oak Hall. As they slowly drive along Allen tells Adam man we sure could have used that $200K. I know, I can tell you this that fuckin Jim Turner and that slut of his Amy are in deep shit.

Allen tell me about Drew Duzz "Dewey", Dayzee's husband. Well you will shit when you meet him. Like I said "he was born and raised right here on the Eastern Shore. He is an only child and inherited this large tract of woodland from his family's estate. The land is hundreds of acres in size and is located between Oak Hall and New Church. Most of it fronts on Rt 13 and a large section borders the Chesapeake Bay. Dewey married our sister Dayzee about fourteen years ago and he worships the ground she walks on. I am sure he would kill any bastard that would touch her.

It's been awhile since you have seen your sister. Yes at least 16-17 years! Well she is a knock out and built like a brick shit house in Georgia. Dewey! He is another story. He is about five feet tall weighs about 120 pounds soaking wet. Most locals call him "Dewey" others call him "Cowboy". You cannot help liking the little bastard as he drips with personality and smiles all the time. He and Dayzee both wear western style clothes plus big ten gallon cowboy hats and fancy cowboy boots.

Dewey and Dayzee own two large profitable businesses. One is considered to be the largest junk yard on the east coast. The other is a large used car dealership. The car dealership borders the junk yard on one side and my ARMA School Building borders it on the other side.

Dayzee manages the Used Car Dealership as an independent business. She proudly states she can get and sell you any car or truck you want for the cheapest price in town if you will allow her the time to do so. OH, by the way the used car business is named "DEWY DUZZ DO CARS"! Funny that's neat!!!!!

Dewey handles the Junk Yard. He advertises he can get you any part for anything made. If he cannot find it they don't make it or you did not need it to start with! He can make and fix anything.

Adam your little sister and her little Dewey are extremely well off, extremely rich to say the least. They live in a beautiful waterfront home on the Chesapeake Bay. They both strongly support our cause and I am very indebted to them both. They are very generous folks. "Praise Be To Allah". They never turn me away when I need help or funds. With the loss of The Rock Cell Depository in the WDR Earthquake funds are in short supply and going to get worse I am afraid.

Adam look up ahead and you can see the 12 feet high fence as it runs along the roadway and surrounds their two businesses. When I see that fence I wonder sometimes if the businesses are legit or just a front, who knows, who cares. Everyone over here on the Eastern Shore loves them both. Damn Allen the fuckin fence runs forever. I know.

Let's go and meet them first before I take you over to my ARMA School Building. Allen turns his old worn out F-150 Ford Truck into the Junk Yard parking area just off the road. As he pulls up and stops Dewey and Dayzee step out on the front porch. Like Allen said "both have smiles that will light up a dark room".

Adam jumps out as Dayzee runs, grabs, hugs and kisses him. They both cry and hug as it has been a long time. Dewey shakes Adam's hand

and tells him to come in and sit a spell. Adam feels great as though he has known Dewey forever. Also his handshake was very firm and strong.

After sitting and chatting in Dewey's office for about forty five minutes Allen tells them he needs to go over to his ARMA school building office to check on a few things and show Adam around. He suggests they meet for supper to continue chatting and talk about old times later. All agree as Allen and Adam leave and drive over to the ARMA School building next door.

Chapter 6

THE LITTLE BRICK SCHOOL HOUSE

Allen drives over to the ARMA School building and pulls into his assigned Parking Place.

The Parking Place Sign Reads "ARMA School Director DR ALLEN RASOUL". He and Adam walk in the Receptionists Office. Allen's secretary Maryrose greets them with a big smile and gives Allen a little peck on the cheek. Allen introduces Adam to Maryrose. Adam thinks to himself "she is stunning and I just bet my AH brother is banging the shit out of her!" Damn I certainly hope so.

Maryrose is the coffee fresh? Yes my dear I just made a new pot. Please bring us both a cup in my office if you will as I plan on showing Adam around the building and the grounds. Yes Sir Mr. ARMA tour guide, they all laugh. Watch him Adam he usually charges twenty five cents a tour but will jack the prices for extras such as coffee. HA! HA! Maryrose you are funny, don't quit your day job.

Coffee in hand Allen tells Adam how the place was a dump when he bought it and that the Accomac County School Board let him have it for a song under the conditions he fix it up or pay too have it torn down and removed. The Interior was nothing special but nicely restored. The old auditorium the Library and the new Marine Biology Laboratory are beautiful. Adam all my instructors are handpicked and highly qualified. Our graduating students receive a full Bachelor's Degree (BS) in Marine Biology after three years of studies. They all have jobs waiting and are in high demand. We graduate on the average between 75-80 students each year. Adam everyone is excited about our upcoming year as we will be specializing in Seafood Farming and related Human Diseases.

Outback and attached to the original old building via a hallway is a large warehouse and storage area. Damn look at the boats. Adam we use these rowboats, kayaks, canoes and small power boats to collect marine sea plant and sea life samples. Most of our studies are hands on; either on the water or in the laboratory. I have never cared for just being a classroom book worm.

Well Adam do you have any questions before we leave? Yes, do you keep all of your ARMA School business separate from your al-Qaida Cell business? Yes indeed, all paperwork and transactions are handled completely as two independent businesses: here and at the farm. All of my/our al-Qaida work is held and discussed in secret at the Cedar View Farm behind locked doors and fences in the SRR. However, we do conduct school work and studies at the farm as a satellite. We launch our boats at various locations, mostly at the farm and Dayzee's place on the Chesapeake Bay. By the way tomorrow I will take you down to our Cedar View Farm piers. I want you to see and go onboard the beautiful pleasure boat I lease; the "ELSA CREE".

Allen what the hell is an "Elsa Cree"? I just told you it's a beautiful pleasure boat, restored in full from an old Log/Buy boat I lease from my neighbors Buddy Cree and his wife Elsa. Their farm borders mine. They are two of the nicest folks you will ever meet, "Born Here's".

One more short question! Fire away. Are you fucking Maryrose? You ass hole (AH), yes indeed every night when I can she lives with me at the farm. You did not see her this morning as she was up and gone before you got up. Anymore smart ass nosy questions! No! As they both laugh. If that's all smart ass let's go and get Maryrose go pick up Dayzee and Dewey and hit the Delmarva Inn Restaurant for a big seafood supper. We have a lot of catching up to take care of. Oh, by the way let Dewey pick up the check, you and I can split the tip. Great let's go!

Maryrose sit up front with your mad lover and I will ride in the back. I just found out you two guys are an item. Adam did I hear you say mad lover you cannot be talking about ole limp dick Allen. HA! HA! As Maryrose and Adam both laugh. You two really think you are funny.

As Allen backs the truck out Adam looks up at the newly painted ARMA school house sign, it reads: "Allen Rasoul Marine Academy" (ARMA). Tears run down his face as he is proud of his kid brother and his success. "Praise Be To Allah".

Chapter 7

THE BEAUTIFUL BOAT

November 03, 2007 Saturday morning. Both Adam and Allen are up early. Adam is still very excited about being over at his brothers Cedar View Farm and is anxious to get assigned to another al-Qaida mission soon. He says to himself "no more of my missions will ever fail, I will die before I let those infidels bastards defeat me again, So Help Me Allah."

Adam let's just eat a light breakfast in the farm house kitchen this morning. Fine with me that big seafood supper last night at the Delmarva Inn Restaurant sure filled me up. Hard to beat fresh seafood that's for sure! Well my man there is no shortage of good seafood over here on the Shore. After breakfast Allen tells Maryrose he and Adam are going to ride over to see Buddy and Elsa Cree as he needs to sign papers to lease their boat the "Elsa Cree" for another year.

As they drive along Adam asks "how far does Buddy live from your place?" His farm borders my place. Actually we could walk but it is still a long way to go as he has a large farm and his house is located on the far side. Allen drives down the road about a mile and turns on to Buddy's driveway. They sure do have a beautiful place. They sure do! As they park and get out of the truck Buddy and Elsa come out to greet them, nice folks.

Good morning guys nice to see you. Folks this is my brother Adam. Nice to meet you Adam, you all come in fresh coffee, butter and biscuits are hot, ready and on the table. Elsa we just ate breakfast but it's no way I will turn down your fresh biscuits they are to die for.

Damn, Buddy driving in I passed your garage and saw your new Ford Club Cab F-150 Truck parked out front. Shit for another dollar I just bet you could have bought a "Red One". Buddy laughs, shit Allen, Elsa said "she wanted it to be Fire Engine Red." You know the rules the gals always win and get what they want you can carry that to the bank.

As they all sit, chat and pig out on fresh hot biscuits Buddy says "Allen I have the boat lease papers here on the desk and all ready for you to sign; same deal as last year. No problem but I still want to buy the boat outright and you still won't sell! No Allen I still cannot bring myself to the point I want to part with it. That old boat has been in my family since the old folks built her right here on this farm back in 1885. My plans are to donate the "Elsa Cree" to one of the local Marine Museums. Probably the Mariners Museum in Newport News, Virginia if they will accept her! There you go Buddy all signed for another year but like I said "if you change your mind my offer still stands." My ARMA students will use it and take excellent care of her forever. I know that, just let me think about it Allen you never know I may change my mind.

Damn Elsa these hot fresh biscuits are terrific! Thank you Adam eat all you want I make a couple dozen every other day from scratch using my mom's old family recipe. Adam quit feeding your fat face and let's get going I have got places to go and things to do and so have these folks. They all laugh as Elsa wraps up a dozen biscuits for Adam to take with him. OK big brother are you satisfied now let's go. Thank you Elsa!

Allen before you leave let me give you a heads up. Sometime right after Thanksgiving I think that is the 22nd Elsa and I will be leaving on our long awaited planned vacation. We plan on driving, taking it slow and stopping when we feel like it. At the present time we are looking at 30 plus days or more who knows. Christmas wherever. God does not care where you celebrate the birth of his son our savior Jesus Christ as long as you just believe in him, TYDL. Adam just thinks to himself "Damn infidel Christians I cannot believe they believe that myth about Jesus Christ and even celebrate Christmas Holidays in his Honor what a joke".

Damn Buddy that's the way to take a vacation. Is there anything you need me to take care of while you are gone? No Allen not really my Uncle Edwin Cree said "he will stop by and check out the place from time to time when he picks up his mail." I will stop the mail and paper deliveries before we leave. Well I will check on things also, I have your CPH number just in case. Thank you Allen that's very kind of you!

As Allen and Adam drive back to the Cedar View Farm Adam asks Allen "what does Buddy do for a living?" Well he worked the "Elsa Cree" as a Waterman and later as an oyster buy boat for years until he had an accident that damaged his back. He is now employed full time with the Chesapeake Bay Bridge Tunnel (CBBT) Authority as a Security Officer.

SOB I knew it, I knew it. Knew what! He stopped me early Thursday morning on the Virginia Beach side of the CBBT when I drove over from Toppers Air Field for a security check. I now remember seeing his uniform name tag "CREE". Allen I will admit he is a nice guy and a good neighbor but he gave me a rough time and really pissed me off Thursday night. Well I certainly hope he did not recognize you that could be a major problem and big trouble. I am sure he did not as Thursday night it was dark, I had my hat tightly pulled down and I was wearing dark sun glasses plus I had long hair and a full beard. Well here is what I want you to do the whole time you are staying here. Keep a low profile, keep your hair cut short, shave every day and dress in casual clothes. Let's just let the dust settle and sit back and see what happens.

Here we are back home as Allen parks the truck. As Adam gets out he notices that the truck has a big Chesapeake Bay Blue Crab Symbol painted on the door with big blue letters "ARMA". That your Academy logo? Yes! Neat, I noticed some folks wearing shirts with "ARMA" printed on them. Now you know! Allen you are something else that's for sure; if mom and dad could only see you now they would be so proud.

Before we go in and discuss my plans for you as I plan on putting your ass to work big time. Let's take a Kubota ride down to the farm piers and ramp area so I can show you the "Elsa Cree". It's a Beautiful Old Boat Elsa and Buddy completely restored. It is now a beautiful pleasure boat complete with berthing cubicles, full galley, a full head, you name it.

There she sits; WOW!!! She is beautiful. Sixty five feet in length over all (LOA), sixteen feet beam (maximum width), draft five feet and weight twenty eight tons, built May, 1885. Allen I can see why you would want to buy and own this beautiful boat.

Meanwhile back at Buddy's: Elsa! Yes dear. I know Allen's brother Adam from somewhere his eyes and his voice. I just cannot put my finger on it. No way dear you just met him for the first time this morning you must be thinking of someone else. Maybe so my dear, maybe so!

Chapter 8

DEWEY'S USED CAR SALES

Upstairs in Allen's study Adam sits back and sips on a cup of coffee as Allen informs him on what his job for the next few weeks, months or years maybe, like it or not. Allen my Delly Rode Cell is a small operation and most of our work up to now has been to raise money to send over to the Far East to support ongoing efforts in Syria. With the loss of The Rock Cell and our Syrian Caliphate Leader Rahism Badhdadi many changes are now taking place and our al-Qaida future movement is in doubt at the present time. We need to rebuild and we need funds.

Adam I run a tight serious ship here at this farm and also up at the ARMA School. We are being watched all the time and we cannot let our guard down for one moment or someone is going to get hurt or worse, killed. Adam I do not take a lot of BS from anyone. Dewey is a nice guy but he does not take a lot of BS from anyone either. We both have loyal people working for us who support our cause to eliminate all infidels. Over here people that betray us over the years have been taken on a boat ride. A boat ride, what does that mean? I'll tell you later, for now let's get to your new job.

Adam your manual job starting Monday morning at 0900Hr will be working at the used car dealership for your sister Dayzee. To save you the commute from here to the Oak Hall area I have arranged for you to move into one of The ARMA Dormitory Rooms that I lease from the Delmarva Inn just across the road. You remember the restaurant where we had supper late last night. By the way most of my students that live there have restaurant meal tickets as I will also provide for you. Any questions! No Sir Lt Allen Rasoul. Adam I do not mean to pull rank on you but I am the Delly Rode Cell Leader and I have a job to do. No worry Allen I know how the game is played and my place. Just do your job for the cause and I will do mine. "Praise Be To Allah". Allen gives Adam a big hug. Great now that we understand each other let's go and check in with your new employer, Sister Dayzee Duzz. What a name!

They depart and drive up to the "DEWEY DUZZ DO CARS" dealership. Allen pulls in parks and they walk in. Well it's about time I have been waiting for you two all morning. Dayzee we did take more time at Buddy Cree's than expected but we made it, here we are. Look Dayzee I briefly brought Adam up to speed on his job with you so I think I will leave you two alone to continue and just go over to the school house and take care of a few things. Fine! Adam I will check back with you later.

Adam get a cup of coffee and follow me. This is going to be you new office. Your job is to help us acquire our cars and trucks. I sell them and take care of all the paper work. Great sis that part of the job was bothering me! Adam close the door sit down and listen very carefully to what I tell you as I explain our automobile operation to you and how it works.

Before I start let me warn you up front that if any of what I tell you gets out on the street Dewey will set up a boat ride for the big mouth involved. You understand that, as I am very serious. Yes! Sis but what do you mean when you use the term "boat ride"? Adam I will make it clear and simple; they dump your dead ass in a fifty five gallon steel drum! They pour in a couple bags of dry concrete mix and put a perforated cap on the drum. They later quietly take you out on the Chesapeake Bay at night for a boat ride and dump your dead fuckin ass overboard. Holy shit Dewey will do that. Dewey has done that, he does not play fuckin games. My little Dewey did not build up this operation working with the Local Mob just to have some AH blow it wide open for him.

Listen up Adam: this is how our used car operation works:
1. We have in place three independent major insurance agencies in the state of Virginia working for us, they are:

(A.) State Auto Insurance of Richmond. POC, Robert Garry.

(B.) Farm Best Auto Insurance of Virginia Beach. POC, Janet Falls.

(C.) Mutual Auto Insurance of Newport News. POC, Paul Papco.

2. When one of their customers has an automobile accident and the damage is severe they

   Investigate the wrecked vehicle declare it a total loss and have it hauled to one of our

   Three nearby salvage yards. They low ball the customer buy the wrecked vehicle and sell

   it too Dewey's Junk Dealership as Junk. They call Dewey; he sends a flatbed truck over

   to the salvage yard picks up the wrecked vehicle and brings it back over here to his Chop

   Shop. There the Chop Shop folks strip it down for used parts.

3. Now here is the beauty part of our operation. The Vehicle Identification Number (VIN) label plate behind the windshield on the left hand side of the dashboard is carefully removed. It is put in an envelope along with the vehicle odometer reading and the new vehicle title showing the car belongs to Dewy. The Division of Motor Vehicles does not know the car has been wrecked and could care less. Adam your new job along with a couple of helpers is to go out to Malls, Shopping Centers, any type of Large Parking Areas and steal a vehicle that matches the wrecked vehicle (If need be we can repaint it here) and bring it back over here. We detail it to match the wreck in every way, change out the VIN Label Plate from the wrecked vehicle adjust the mileage and there you have it a new used car for sale on our lot for a good price. I settle up with the insurance agent on his low ball check to the customer plus a little bonus for his time and support. Note: I also keep a record of the original owners name so we do not accidently sell this vehicle to them for obvious reasons as they may remember and recognize the VIN.

Adam go and check out our used car lot. All of the cars and trucks are top of the line and they are beautiful. Other dealers buy from us and wonder where we can find such nice units to sell. Hell Adam we get our money back from the chopped used parts; most of the time from the sale of the engine and the transmission alone.

Dayzees phone rings. Hello, Hi Janet, yes you have us a totally wrecked new Ford F-150 at our Virginia Beach location. Great we will pick it up later this week. Thank you my dear. Damn, there you go Adam keep your eyes open for a new Ford F-150 Club Cab truck. Piece a cake.

Well if you do not have any more questions let's go walk around. I will show you the rest of our used car dealership e.g. the maintenance, washing, detailing, oil changing, painting, tires you name it. We service all of our vehicles before we put them on the lot, nothing is over looked. Sis I can see that, they are all beautiful vehicles.

Chapter 9

A STARTLING SURPRISE VISIT

November 21, 2007. Wednesday morning. Ring, Ring hello ARMA, Maryrose here how may I help you? Maryrose this is Dewey, is Allen in his office? Yes he is! Please let me speak with him! I will click you over. Doc it's Dewey. Good morning Dewey you are on the job early as always. Happy early "Thanksgiving"! Thank you same to you! Make sure you; Maryrose and Adam come over for Dayzee's usual big thanksgiving Feast tomorrow evening. Do not worry we will be there we cannot miss that.

Look, what I called you about is I have two very excited gentlemen sitting here in my office that are anxious to come over and see you. Who are they and what do they want? They just laugh at me and will not say. They just want to come over and see you and Adam and surprise you both. Hell Dewey I do not have time for fun and games this is my catch up time as most of our students are off for the Thanksgiving Holiday. I know. Shit Dewey send them on over, I will take a break and speak with them.

Fellers Allen is very busy but he told me to send you on over. His office is just across the parking lot in that Old School Building. You can leave your car parked here and walk over. Just go over and walk on in his secretary's office it is just inside she will call Allen for you.

They walk in as Allen is at the door to meet them. He looks at the two men and recognizes them right away although it's been years. He screams and almost pisses his pants.

Praise be and Glory Be to Allah as I live and breathe. It is you "Rahism" all news reports and feedback from the Wood Duck Ridge (WDR) Earthquake destruction listed you and Jamil as killed. All three men hug and cry with joy, so wonderful to see you both what a surprise.

Maryrose please come in here and meet our Kunar Supreme Caliphate Commander Rahism Badhdadi and his right hand man Sargent Jamil. Maryrose is as excited as Allen as they honor this man as a true al-Qaida God and Leader. They cannot believe he is standing there in person. She cries and gives each of them a big hug, what an honor to meet you both.

Allen says please come in to my office and sit down we have so much to talk about. Maryrose call Adam, Dayzee and Dewey and tell them to come over here PDQ and also put on more coffee if you will. Yes my dear!

Adam walks in and he cannot believe his eyes. Where in the hell did you two POS come from? Did you just fall from the sky above? They all laugh as the ice is broken and the dust settles between old longtime friends. In walk Dewey and Dayzee. They of course do not know Rahism or Jamil as introductions take place. What a pleasure to meet you both. What a surprise as all reports listed you both as being lost in the WDR Earthquake. Allen looks at Rahism and asks him to fill them all in on just what happened over there how did you two survive? Well it's a long story let me start from the beginning.

Allen as you and Adam know I called for and set up Major Meetings at "The Rock Cell" that included all eight of my Afghanistan al-Qaida Cell Leaders starting on November 5th to go over and complete our plans for the Big al-Qaida Syrian Offensive. All went well no problems.

Your dear brother Abraham "The Rock Cell" Commander was a gracious host. Sad to say he was lost in the WDR Earthquake. Praise Be to Allah! Your brother was a powerful force and a wonderful al-Qaida leader. He will be solely missed and will be praised by Allah forever.

To continue as luck would have it for Jamil and me and with the meetings progressing so well we completed most of our work well ahead of schedule. That being the case I decided to let everyone off for a long weekend. I was staying at the outside park Ranger Cottage as a guest of Jamil. On the 9th of November last Friday when the WDR Earthquake erupted this cottage was spared and Jamil and I survived. Praise Be To Allah.

Folks that WDR Earthquake was a terrible experience and a terrible sight to behold! I can never remember anything like it before, it was so overwhelming! In the far distance you could see this huge bubble start to develop around the entire Stone Mountain Range that contained a white hot glow. Within minutes the entire Stone Mountain Range was engulfed and started to crumble within itself and just disappear. The heat generated was so intense most of the surrounding rock glazed over like sheets of molted glass.

Rahism begins to cry. Folks we lost everything all of our supplies, weapons, billions of U.S. dollars we had and were still moving in from the Medcalf Hospital Bank Depository in Jalalabad and worst of all thousands of highly trained soldiers, martyrdoms and support personnel. All is gone absolutely nothing remains as aftershocks still continue to this day. It is devastating to our cause but we must continue to rebuild and start over. "Praise Be to Allah", we will not give in and let these Christian and Jewish Infidels consume us.

Allen you Adam and Abraham trained at "The Rock Cell back in the early years and that was when I first met you three guys. We worked hard, supplied, built and kept: The Rock Cell" a top secret base all these years just to lose it to a force of nature. Local infidel slaves working at The Rock Cell would tell us from time to time that their so called God would rain destruction upon us. Could they be correct? Praise Be To Allah, I say no! Their God is false and a myth, it could not happen. Folks the bottom line is we will not give up our fight our cause. Syria will be ours. We will conquer Syria and make it a major al-Qaida Caliphate someday, somehow and someway.

Anyway lucky for us Jamil had a MC at the cottage with about $100K remaining. We packed this up along with other supplies we needed and with one old horse drawn cart wagon hit the trail disguised as roadies and headed for Jalalabad. From there we made our way over to Baghdad. With help from many al-Qaida fractions along the way we ended up as planned in Santiago Cuba. Our short stay in Cuba was a break I will discuss with you later. From Cuba we caught a very expensive pleasure boat owned by a local drug dealer and landed somewhere in the Florida Keys. We rented a car and drove up here late last night and got a room over at the Delmarva Inn, you know the rest of the story.

Folks I need to take a break I will fill you in on more details later. My good friends; Jamil and I have been on the run since November the 9ᵗʰ with little or no let up. Both of us are two worn out old men. Before I close and let you go I would like to ask you all "at this time just treat Jamil and me as two old friends up from Florida on a visit and not let anyone know our true identities or where we actually came from". In public call me Ralph Rasoul and call Jamil Jim."

Rahism as an extra safety measure when we finish here may I suggest this! Let me take both of you back over to the Delmarva Inn and get you reregister in to our ARMA Dormitory Area as full time ARMA students along with student Restaurant meal tickets. Dayzee and Adam can take your rental vehicle back to the rental agency and turn it in for you. For the remainder of the day you guys can settle in get some sleep and rest up. That sounds great Allen thank you so much. Any questions!

Yes Dayzee what is it! Do not forget everyone in this room is invited to our home tomorrow evening for our big annual "Thanksgiving Day" celebration feast. The feast will start around 1600Hr but come early if you like. Yes Allen! Rahism like I told Adam earlier while you are staying here on the "Shore" you guys need to keep your hair cut short, shave every day, continue to wear casual clothes and keep a low profile. Thank you Allen we will do just that. Any more questions, if not and if you do not mind, folks I would like to call it a day as Jamil and I need to get some much needed rest and take Allen's advice and generous offer.

Maryrose goes back to work as all the others leave. Allen also leaves and takes Jamil and Rahism on over to the Delmarva Inn to get them rechecked and settled in as discussed. As they ride over, Rahism asks Allen "did you receive my last coded text from The Rock Cell that I sent you? Was that the text speaking to the Exoset Missile as being High Priority! Yes that's the one. Allen we must get that Exoset Missile information in order to continue on.

Well Rahism once we heard you were killed in the WDR Earthquake I was not sure I needed to continue investigating this. However something told me to continue and as we speak I have put some plans in place I will discuss with you later. Wonderful!

Allen we need that weapon to rebuild; guns and bullets will not get the job done anymore. Remember in Afghanistan we are starting completely over again from zero. Allen I want that Syrian Caliphate; we need it in order to conquer our Far East Goals that's the bottom line.

Allen I will let you in on a secret plan we are working on. When Jamil and I came over and went through Santiago Cuba it was a planned stop over so as to meet with my Cuban al-Qaida Cell leader Lt Ramey Sanchez. He has a lot of authority in Cuba and commands the only al-Qaida Cell we have formed in that Country. Lt Ramey Sanchez is in close contact with a local Neo-Nazi Order. They have a strong foot hold in Cuba and are willing to work with us to support our cause as they dislike the Jews as much as we dislike Christians, Jews and any Infidels that do not support our cause. Allen this Neo-Nazi Order needs and wants this Exoset Missile Weapon as much as we do to continue their elimination movements and programs.

Allen here is the strong part of the whole deal, Lt Ramey Sanchez tells me that the Neo-Nazi Order has the facilities underground in Santiago Cuba that can manufacture and produce operational missiles and drones. Allen get me all the Exoset information you can find, anything at all just get it. Yes Sir I will do my best!

Here we are as Allen gets Rahism and Jamil all rechecked in at the Delmarva Inn. Go get some sleep and rest I will pick you up tomorrow about 1500Hr to go over to Dayzee's and Dewey's home for Thanksgiving dinner it will be second to none that's for sure. On the way back to his office Allen cannot think about anything but what Rahism said to him "GET ME ALL THAT EXOSET MISSILE INFORMATION YOU CAN FIND, JUST GET IT"!!!!!

Chapter 10

THE DELLY RODE CELL SPECIAL
SECRET MEETING

November 26, 2007 Monday morning early. Maryrose please call Rahism, Jamil, Adam, Hess and Baka tell them to attend a meeting at the Squadron Ready Room (SRR) at the Barn about 2000HR. Tell Hess to call Nanki and Manki and bring them along also. Yes my dear, anything else? No that ought to cover it for now.

Later Allen at his Cedar View Farm Barn about 1945Hr Is going down his invited list of al-Qaida agents that he had Maryrose notify. All are present and on time except Nanki, that little bastard for some reason is always late. If he does not straighten his little ass up he may just find himself taking a fuckin boat ride; HA! HA!

All in place Allen starts the meeting. Good evening guy's I called this special meeting so we can start planning and putting together plans for our next Mission here at our Cell "The Delly Rode". I have been working on this Exoset Missile Mission alone since I was ordered by our leader Rahism Badhdadi back in early November. When we received the sad news that Rahism was lost in the WDR Earthquake I put this mission on the back burner as a low priority item until now.

The door of the SRR slowly opens and in walks Nanki with a very sheepish red faced grin on his face. Allen stirs right through him with glowing eyes and says "good evening Nanki so glad that your fuckin little ass could finally make our very important special meeting"!!!! Doc, please forgive me I got so involved with some sea life samples at the ARMA School Lab I completely lost track of the time. Well sit your ass down I will deal with you later.

Where was I? You were interrupted as you stated "our new mission was a low priority item until now"! Oh yes, thank you Hess. When I said until now, because Thanks Be To Allah our Caliphate Leader is alive and well and with us tonight. Rahism please stand and be recognized. Guys for the grace of Allah meet your Supreme Commander Rahism Badhdadi and his second in command Sargent (Sgt) Jamil. Everyone stands they salute walk by and give Rahism and Jamil a hug and the traditional greeting kiss on the cheek.

With all the introductions and traditional greetings over Allen continues. Gentlemen our new High Priority Mission here at our Delly Rode Cell is to obtain or at least gather any information we can find on the new U.S. Military Weapon the Exoset Missile Program. Rahism would you please take the stand and explain this mission and set in place some plans for us. I will continue and state my progress on this mission later when you are complete.

Rahism steps up! They all look at this large man and realize he is a man of no nonsense and is very serious about the al-Qaida cause. His reputation is well known. Gentlemen first let's get one thing straight up front. While I am here please treat me as an equal. I am just another al-Qaida soldier like you; Allen Rasoul leads this Delly Rode Cell I work for him as you do. I fight for the cause as I strongly believe in it. All infidels are either with us or against us. Those that oppose us are to be eliminated, bottom line, enough said!

Rahism continues; the recent meetings we held at WDR "The Rock Cell" tell us that we can no longer accomplish our planned missions with foot soldiers on the ground and small arms fire. Since the Allies are using advanced weapons on our bases e.g. Drones, Missiles, etc we need to obtain, train and use these same type weapons on our enemies the infidels.

Gentlemen that WDR Earthquake reduced our Far East Operation to Zero! We have nothing left and are financially bankrupted. We must start over and rebuild and it starts right here in this SRR with your Cell

"The Delly Rode". Gentlemen Get Me That Exoset Missile any way you can. When I say get me an Exoset Missile I realize that maybe impossible. However please get me all the information you can gather on this weapon; plans, technical manuals, CPU read outs, Computer Aided Design (CAD) CD, three dimensional read outs (3-DI), anything you can just get it so we can get our rebuilding programs started ASAP.

On our trip over from Afghanistan Jamil and I had a planned layover in Santiago Cuba. While there we met with our Cuban Cell leader Lt Ramey Sanchez. Lt Ramey Sanchez to add support to our Cuban cause is working with the Neo-Nazi German Army (NNGA). This NNGA Order is well established underground throughout Cuba. The NNGA leader is Adolf H. Goring his second in command is Adolf H. Junker. If you have studied any "World War Two" history at all you will find that these two NNGA leaders have famous fathers that led German Forces under the Command of the famous German Nazi leader Adolf Hitler. As you can see both of these men named their first born sons after Adolf Hitler, in his honor!

Lt Ramey Sanchez told us that the NNGA has a secret location that has the capabilities to manufacture drones and missiles if we can just get them the necessary Software Information they need. Can we do this? We must try it's our only hope to survive. "Praise Be To Allah."

Gentlemen, fellow al-Qaida Agents your Cell "The Delly Rode" led by my long standing friend Allen Rasoul is the only fully functional al-Qaida Cell remaining in the U.S.A. as we speak. We have fractions with scattered members throughout but no fully organized Cells with firm leadership.

Gentleman you must step up be leaders and help support the cause to rebuild. "Praise Be To Allah".

Allen that's all I have for now, please take over and present your progress on the Exoset Missile Program Mission.

Fellows it's getting late let's all call it a night and let's all meet back here tomorrow night at 2000Hr and we can continue to discuss our new Exoset Missile Mission. At that time I will bring you up to date on my progress so far. Also I want to discuss another Mission I have been working on for years I will present to you at this meeting. Good night and remember nothing said tonight leaves this SRR!

Chapter 11

A TRAGIC SHORT VACATION

November 26, 2007, Monday evening about 2000Hr. Buddy and Elsa Cree have loaded up their brand new Ford F-150 Club Cab Pickup truck and are almost ready to leave and start out on their long awaited vacation. One last thing before we leave Elsa; let me call and touch base with Uncle Edwin Cree and let him know we are finally leaving at long last.

Hello! Uncle Ed this is Buddy I thought I would call one last time to let you know Elsa and I are packed, ready and finally pulling out to start our long awaited vacation. Damn you sure are getting a late start. I know, but driving this late up through Delaware traffic conditions are not that bad and we are not in any big hurry to start with. Uncle Ed I stopped the Newspapers and mail deliveries. You know where the house keys are hidden plus I gave you a set of keys years ago. Yes, I still have them right here on my old key chain. No worry Buddy I will drive over from time to time to check on things when I go over to pick up my mail at the Exmore Post Office. Stay safe you and Elsa have a nice trip and enjoy yourselves. Thank you sir, we will; we love you. I love you too, good bye!

As Elsa and Buddy leave and drive they approach Allen Rasoul's Cedar View Farm driveway entrance. Damn the front gate is wide open that's a first it's always closed and locked. I think I will drive on in and give Allen a key to the house as discussed. Buddy do not do that just put the key in the metal box mounted on the gate like you told him you would do and let's just go, we are already getting a late start. Hell Elsa, it will only take a minute that way I know for sure he got the key OK!

Buddy drives through the open gate and down the long very dark driveway towards Allen's old farm house. He pulls up beside the fence just outside the old Barn parking area across from the house turns off his lights and shuts off the engine. As he gets out of his truck he looks around and sees a light and hears sounds coming from the Old Barn. He walks over try's the gate latch leading to the barn, it opens. He walks in, no one in sight. I will be a SOB, there parked beside the fence is the very same old 1941 Packard Hearse I stopped late Halloween Night on the Virginia Beach side of the CBBT. Buddy continues to walk around the old Hearse and check it out; the North Carolina license plate number he remembers checks out. North Carolina, "Wilson No. 1". That's the same Terrorist Plate Number we received over the scanner from the Middlesex County Sheriff's Department (MCSD) and the Virginia State Police (VASP) "All Points Bulletin" report. Suspected driver named Adam Rasoul "a person of interest". Like I told Elsa "I knew I recognized that voice from somewhere".

Buddy continues to walk around and stumble in the darkness. As he investigates he thinks to himself "what the hell have I discovered here at Allen's farm." He an Elsa have known Allen for a long time now and they have become good friends and great neighbors. They have always been a little suspect of Allen and his strange demeanor at times but Allen being so brilliant in his Marine field and the longtime director of the ARMA they realize his type of people trend to act weird a bit flaky and fucked up at times.

Buddy stops and listens, nothing but dead silence, he turns to leave as he knows he must report finding the Old Packard Hearse and God only knows what else to the Accomac County Sheriff's Department (ACSD) and Sheriff George Bowden PDQ. He takes out his CPH and presses the ACSD listed cell phone number. Hello, ACSD how may I help you Mr. Cree! Is Sheriff Booow!!!! Bam! As Hess comes up from behind and strikes him hard over the head with a baseball bat. Buddy collapses to the concrete apron badly injured. Buddy's CPH still on, sounds off loudly "Mr. Cree are you still there, are you still there" then buzzes as it goes silent.

Allen upstairs in his old farm house apartment he and Maryrose share is getting prepared for bed as his CPH rings. Damn Maryrose who in the hell can that be at this time of night. He sees on the screen it is Hess and picks up. Hess what the fuck do you want? Do you know what time it is? Hell we just adjourned our meeting I get upstairs get ready for bed and you call what's wrong now? Doc we have got big problems I stayed over to clean up the SRR, shut down all the lights and lockup. As I walked out I ran across an outside visitor snooping around.

Hess who is this visitor do we know him? Yes sir, he is our neighbor Buddy Cree. Doc we may have problems as he was on his CPH calling the ACSD as I discovered him and took him out. Hess do not let him out of your sight for one minute I will be right down.

As Hess hangs up his CPH he looks around and here comes Elsa Cree running up and screaming as she sees her husband Buddy injured and lying on the concrete. What have you done to my husband you bastard as she screams and begins to strike out at Hess! Hess steps back and swings the baseball bat hitting and knocking Elsa to the ground out cold.

Allen walks up but he is too late to prevent Hess from striking Elsa. Holy Shit Hess what the hell are we going to do here this late at night and how in the hell did these two get in here? Doc I do not know, some AH left the front gate wide open and the barn gate unlocked.

SOB, now what! Hess it had to be Nanki he was running late to our meeting and you know how absent minded that little bastard gets when he is in a hurry! Damn Allen what do we do now? Hess sad to say we have no choice our al-Qaida cause and our missions come first and as nice as the Cree's are they are still low life Christian Infidels.

Hess no one is around to see or hear any of this as they all left right after the meeting a while ago. Hess get the Kubota, two fifty five gallon drums, four bags of concrete mix and two large storage bags from the Barn Store Room. Yes Sir! Hess you know the routine same process as before; put their bodies in the storage bags, shoot them, tie the bags tightly closed, take them down to the boat ("Elsa Cree"), load everything onboard, dump each one in a drum, pour two bags of concrete mix in to each drum and tap on the drum lids. Piece a cake Doc!!!!

Let's see Hess it's so late now, just wait until Sunrise tomorrow morning to take the drums out on the Chesapeake Bay to dump them over board. Hess tomorrow morning after you return from dumping the Cree drums overboard drive Buddy's new Ford F-150 truck to "Dewey Duzz Do Cars

Dealership". When you get there drive on around the back and park it in the Detail Shop to keep it out of sight. Go in and tell Dayzee to clean it out and destroy all the luggage, detail the truck in its entirety and take care of all the necessary arrangements and paper work selling the truck to me. She knows exactly what to do. Yes Sir!

Hess do you want me to stay and give you a hand? Nope Doc, I can handle this little job as usual routine, besides I love eliminating low life fuckin infidels. Doc go in the house get a hot shower and go to bed it's been a long tiring day for everyone. Thanks Hess good night! Good night Doc!

As Allen slowly walks back to the house he thinks to himself "Hess is right, eliminating Infidels can be a pleasure". Just think Buddy and Elsa Cree buried at sea from the stern of their beloved beautiful boat "The Elsa Cree". How great is that! "Praise Be To Allah".

Chapter 12

RED TRUCK BLUE TRUCK

November 27, 2007 Tuesday morning early. Hess is just returning from his burial at sea duties taking care of the Cree's as he secures the Elsa Cree's spring lines to the pier pilings. He takes his time to stop and look out at the beautiful sunrise and smell the fresh salt air, what a wonderful day. He thinks to himself what's my next job as there is always something around this place that needs to be taken care of that's for damn sure.

Hell I might as well go ahead and drive Buddy Cree's Ford F-150 on up to "Dewey Duzz Do Cars" Dealership and like Doc said "have Dayzee detail it and get it all squared away" That should be a piece of cake.

Hess looks at Buddy's new Ford F-150 Club Cab, it sure is pretty but I would have gotten a blue one instead of red. He gets in and drives it down the Cedar View Farm driveway, slows down and automatically opens the front gate. He drives through and stops at the Nandua Roadway. He looks back and checks to make sure the gate is closed and locked then looks both ways and starts to pull out.

Meanwhile earlier; Uncle Edwin Cree is leaving the Exmore Post Office Parking lot after getting his mail and decides at the last minute; what the hell I am this close to Buddy's farm I just as well drop by gleam what's left of the garden and pick up those 2x4 wood studs he has stored in the barn he said I could have and check the place out.

As uncle Ed drives down Nandua Roadway he approaches the Cedar View farm entrance. He looks over and sees this new Ford F-150 Ford truck waiting to pull out he slows down and waves as he passes by. As he continues to drive on to Buddy's farm he slows down and slams on his brakes. Holy Shit, I am sure that the Virginia State license plate on the front of that truck read "BECREE".

Uncle Ed quickly pulls his truck in to Buddy's driveway and turns around. He speeds up and chases down the other truck but is careful not to get to close and alert the driver. He gets just close enough so he can clearly read the rear License Plate; sure enough it reads "BECREE". SOB that's Buddy's fuckin new Ford F-150 Truck! What the hell is going on?

Uncle Ed being an old man in his early eighties is in no position to force a pull over to investigate and ask the driver any questions so he decides to just follow the truck for a while at this time. He wonders where in the hell are Elsa and Buddy they just left late yesterday on their planned vacation. What the Hell is going on. He begins to worry and is completely confused. He thinks he should pull over and call the ACSD but he does not want to take a chance and lose sight of Buddy's truck so he just follows closely along for the time being.

Hess continues to drive on and turns on to The Delly Rode, State Rt 13 up towards the New Church area. Uncle Ed continues to follow for what seems like hours finally Hess slows and turns into the "Dewey Duzz Do Cars" Dealership. Hess carefully pulls up to a side gate, opens the gate and drives through and closes the gate behind him. He drives on down the lane and pulls the truck into a garage that's labeled "Vehicle Detail & Paint Shop" and parks.

Uncle Ed still very confused also pulls in to the far side of the dealership out front and parks his truck. Becoming very upset he is not sure what to do next so he decides to call the ACSD and talk with Sheriff George Bowden. Hello Sheriff Bowden how can I help you. Sheriff this is Ed, Ed. Ed, Creeeee!!!! Ed for Christ sake calm down what the hell is the matter? Sheriff I am at the "Dewey Duzz Do Cars" Dealership and I think we have problems can you drive over and meet me here I need your help? Yes Ed I will drive over just calm down before you have the big one in front of God and everybody. Ed right now I am at the Wallops Island Space Center Complex (WISC) closing out an investigation I will meet you at Dewey's in about one hour. Ok George do the best you can just get here ASAP I will be waiting for you.

Knowing the Sheriff will arrive soon Ed begins to calm down somewhat and decides to go in the front office and enquire about the truck and find out what's going on. He opens the front door walks in and right away sees Dayzee. Dayzee sees Ed and greets him with a big smile and says "Edwin Cree you old PAS long time no see where the hell have you been keeping yourself".

Dayzee this is not a social visit I am a very upset old man! Dayzee unaware about any of these related truck problem asks Ed what in the hell is the matter? Dayzee where is my nephew Buddy and his wife Elsa Cree and what is their new truck doing here at your dealership! Ed I do not have a fuckin clue about what you are talking about, just calm down. Well somebody better start talking I want to get to the bottom of this! I want answers and I want answers now! Dayzee what the hell is my nephews new Ford truck doing here at this dealership and what has happened to him and Elsa? Buddy and I bought our new Ford trucks the same day at the same place and I now know you have his truck here as I followed it all the way up from Exmore and watched it turn in here now what the fuck is going on. Ed I still do not know what you are talking about. SOB, when Sheriff Bowden gets here he will settle this problem, he is on the way so somebody around here better start talking and I mean now I am tired of this fuckin BS!!!!!!!!!

Hess having heard Ed Cree's loud voice coming from the front office when he walked up is standing in the hallway behind the office door. He has seen enough and heard enough and knows he must take some type of defensive action. Hess waits and just as Ed turns his back to the hallway door he steps through walks over and strikes the old man severely over the head with a baseball bat. Dayzee jumps back still unaware at what is going on and screams at Hess; "Hess what the fuck is going on why was that old man so pissed off and upset about some damn truck problem?"

Hess finally calms Dayzee down and tells her all about Buddy Cree's intrusion and trespassing on the Cedar View Farm last night and the necessary defensive actions he and Allen decided they had to take. Old man Ed Cree just accidently rode by and saw me driving the Cree Truck this morning; he evidently recognized it and followed me up here.

SOB Hess we need to act fast this old bastard is trouble and he screamed that the Sheriff may be on the way over here. Hess is he dead? Yes I think so I hit him very hard, yes he is gone. Hess let's drag his dead ass down the hallway and dump him in the Utility Closet for the time being. Go out front and drive his new blue Ford F-150 Truck around back to the "Vehicle Detail & Paint Shop" and park it next to Buddy's truck that you just drove up in from the farm.

Get going Hess move quickly, get a move on! Yes mam! If and when the Sheriff arrives if he comes at all you and Adam stay in the rear of the building and keep a low profile. Just let me handle the Sheriff alone by myself. Great, no problem!

As Hess gets ready to drive Ed Cree's truck around back Adam finally walks in, late again. Dayzee looks at him and states "you AH late again". Sorry my dear little sister I over slept, I stayed at the Farm last night and had to drive all the way up here. No Shit! Adam can see and tell Dayzee is upset about something and that he better be walking on eggs for a while. Adam I am upset and I do not have time to explain anything to you now and I do not need any more BS! Adam just go on in the back check in with Hess he can update you on what has happened this morning around this fuckin place.

Adam when you see Hess tell him to go over to Dewey's storage area and get a steel fifty five gallon drum, two bags of concrete mix and take care of old man Cree's body. Hess knows the routine and what to do. You and him can take the drum out to sea and drop it overboard later tonight. OK, OK, my dear just calm down everything is going to be alright. Get going! Yes mam!

As Adam leaves to go and check in with Hess; as expected the Accomac County Sheriff drives up parks and walks in. Dayzee now somewhat calmed down has her story in place and has anticipated some of the questions he may ask her should he drop by.

Sheriff George Bowden you old PAS long time no see, what brings your beautiful face to my humble door. He laughs, Dayzee you are a piece of work that's for sure as he gives her a big hug. Dayzee how have you been you are gorgeous as usual? How is your little Cowboy Dewey? I am doing fine and Dewey is doing great. He still is able to "ring my bell and make the Partridges Fly", HA! HA! George are you getting any hay for your donkey? Not as much as I would like too, why are you missing any? No, Dewey keeps the hay loft full, HA! HA!

Damn George this is the first time I have seen you dressed in your New Style County uniform; I read about them and saw your pictures in the

Newspaper. Pretty snazzy! Shit George it looks like with the new uniform you would at least polish your damn badge sometime. Well I tell you what come over tonight and polish it for me and when you finish you can do my badge next! Fuckin cute George, you are so bad as they both laugh.

Dayzee all joking aside and on a more serious note I came by here to meet old man Edwin Cree. He called from here earlier and said he had some serious problems he needed to talk with me about He sounded very upset and could hardly speak. He was so upset he did not say what the problems were about. I told him to stay put that I would come by and meet him here ASAP Have you by chance seen him I did not see his new Ford truck out front anywhere? George it's been so long since I have seen that nice old gentleman, I cannot remember when. Shit he used to stop by all the time when he worked up at the WISC Complex but since he has retired he just stays south in the Exmore area; he was like another father to me and Dewey. Are you sure he said for you to meet him here. Yes, I could be wrong but I am sure he said here. Well if he came by here he must have stayed in his truck parked outside, got bored waiting and decided to leave. Maybe his problems went away. Anyway like I said "I have not seen him in ages".

Well Dayzee let me run I have things I need to take care of, if you see Ed Cree tell him to stay put and call me. George I will do just that, nice to see you again, please poke your head in the door sometime when you drive by. Will do, good bye, tell Dewey hello for me.

As Sheriff Bowden leaves Hess and Adam walk into Dayzee front office. She looks at them and say's "fellows that was close, too fuckin close we need to be more cautious or we are going to drop our guard and someone is going to get hurt around here. How about old man Ed Cree's body! We have it all secured in a steel drum and ready for a boat ride later tonight. Great!

Now listen up, here is what I want you two to do; Hess take and put the drum in one of Allen's ARMA small trucks with the School logo on the door and drive it slowly back to the Cedar View Farm and load it onboard the Elsa Cree. You and Adam can take it out on the Cheasepeake Bay and dump it overboard later tonight after your SRR Secret 2000Hr Meeting. For now Adam you remain here and mine the store. E- Mail and Phone all our local Auto Insurance POC and tell them to find me two brand new wrecked Ford F-150 Club Cab pickup trucks ASAP. I need those wrecked trucks to chop, their titles and their VIN labels so I can move our two new trucks we just put in stock ASAP. While you are at it get off your fat fuckin ass and sell a few vehicles our front lot is getting over stocked. They all laugh!!!

Right now fellows I am going to go over to the ARMA school office and sit down and have a long discussion with Allen and Maryrose and bring them up to date on the problems we have encountered over here this morning. Do either of you have any questions! No! Good. One last thing, keep your eyes and ears open because that dip shit Sheriff we have employed by this County will probably come back snooping around once old man Ed Cree and his truck are officially reported missing.

Chapter 13

THE EXOSET MISSILE MEETING

November 27, 2007. Tuesday evening about 1900Hr, Allen Rasoul arrives at the SRR in the Barn. When he walks in he breaks out into aloud laugh as he sees Nanki sitting right up front fresh as a daisy ready for this important meeting to begin. Glad to see you here on time for a change Nanki that's more like it. Thank you sir!

About 1945Hr all the other invited al-Qaida agents begin to walk in; Rahism, Jamil, Adam, Hess, Baka and Manki. Allen looks around and says for a change it looks like all are present on time and accounted for, how nice. Everyone looks at Nanki and laughs. A good start for any meeting let's proceed!

Gentlemen I will do my best to keep this meeting as short as possible so please listen up as I will need all of your input and support on this Exoset Missile Mission. Like I said to some of you earlier I have done research work upfront on this Exoset Missile Mission since I received a texted message from Rahism Badhdadi.

To update you all that may not realize this; the Exoset Missile is now the most advanced non- nuclear weapon in the U.S. Military Arsenal at this time. All reports we are able to receive from inside Dekamp Aviation

Engineering (DAE) tell us that progress is well ahead of schedule thanks to a young aeronautical engineer they now have employed there named Cedric Fauntleroy. Rumors throughout the field say he is an Aviation genius.

This young twenty two year old man has saved the DAE Company and most of all the entire U.S. Military Exoset Missile program. His knowledge and expertise quickly developed and solved the missile fuel, range and guidance control problems. The remaining work left on the program is to fully test the two operational Prototype Exoset missiles. Where and when these scheduled tests will take place is unknown to us at this time.

Our inside al-Qaida agents employed by Nellis Air Force Base and Albert Edward Aerodrome (AEA) in Las Vegas where DAE is located were able to get a qualified agent of ours hired full time by DAE. She is our secret inside POC. All the feedback I have received thus far is in coming through her, and I might add she is doing one hell of a job for our cause.

Jamil you may remember her as she received most of her al-Qaida training at "The Rock Cell" under your command. Her full name is Anna Belle. She is a beautiful blue eyed blonde beauty from right here in nearby Williamsburg, Virginia. Allen I do remember her well in more ways than one if you know what I mean, they all laugh. If I recall she was badly injured in a hand grenade training exercise doing her training period and lost a finger. That's her!

Well the latest texted information from her which I just received yesterday is that the DAE planned Exoset Missile tests may take place right here in our backyard at the Wallops Island Space center Complex (WISC) Wallops Island, Virginia sometime in January of next year. Hell Allen that would be great, like you said "that's right here in our backyard" and besides that we now have one of our best agents employed there full time. Hess you got it, keep your fingers crossed that this will happen. Guys give me your feedback on this ASAP.

Putting the Exoset Missile Mission aside for now let me throw this at you and put it all on the table! These low life infidels working at the WISC Complex over the years have developed and tested weapons that are now being used by the Allies to kill our innocent people all over the World as we speak in the name of peace. BS!

Hear this and think about it and let it sink in! My Dream Mission for our al-Qaida "Delly Rode Cell" is to completely take out and destroy the WISC Complex, just take it down in its entirety reduce it to ashes. Can we do this? Like I said just think about this and give me your feedback. If the Exoset Missile tests were held at the WISC Complex maybe with some very careful planning we could intercept the Exoset Missile Information we so badly need and at the same time attack and destroy the WISC. Think about that!!! Any questions at this time! If no questions that's all I have for you tonight at this time. Please give me your thoughts and feedback on these missions ASAP.

One unrelated question Doc! Yes Manki go ahead. While I was getting ready for bed last night I thought I heard a disturbance out near the barn parking area. When I looked out all I saw was Hess getting in the Kubota to drive off somewhere. Doc did you see or hear anything? Manki we did have a slight problem take place late last night right after our meeting but Hess and I took care of it right away. It was minor nothing any of you people need to know or worry about.

Anymore questions! If not this meeting is adjourned. For now just go back to your regular jobs, keep a low profile and send me your feedback too support our planned missions. Adam, Hess and Nanki hang around for a minute longer I need to speak with you three in private.

After the others leave and the SRR is cleared Adam says "What's up Doc! Who the hell are you "Bugs Bunny", HA! HA! Get serious Adam and listen up! After the meeting last night we had some unexpected visitors. We did? Yes! Who were they and what did they want? Wait just a minute and I will tell you all about it. First, Nanki these visitors were trespassing and came in because you carelessly left the front gate open and the barn gate unlocked. I know Doc, I thought about that while I was sitting here in the SRR. Well I will overlook it this time but if it ever happens again your little ass will be in deep shit, do you understand me! Yes Sir! Now get your fuckin ass out of here and go back to work. Yes SIR!!!!!

Adam as you was asking the two unexpected visitors last night were our neighbors Elsa and Buddy Cree. Holy Shit! Nanki left the front gate wide open and they drove right on in. Buddy Cree saw your 1941 Packard Hearse and recognized it right off. As luck would have it Hess caught him in time just as he was calling the ACSD and took him out! Great, I did not like the little SOB to start with plus he really pissed me off when he stopped me on the Virginia Beach side of the CBBT Halloween night.

What happened to Elsa Cree? Well she came running up, screaming like crazy so Hess had to eliminate her also. That's a fuckin shame I sure am going to miss her fresh baked biscuits, HA! HA! Hell Adam they were nice folks but still low life infidel **POS** fighting against our cause. I know! Where are they now? Hess took them out on the Chesapeake Bay early this morning for one of our famous boat rides and deep sixth both of them. What a shame!

You two get the hell out of here I have things to take care of up at the ARMA School House. By the way Dayzee came over this morning and told me and Maryrose about the problems you all had with old man Edwin Cree at the car dealership. Yes we know! As a matter of fact we are going down to the boat at this time to take Old Man Edwin Cree on his last boat ride. If we keep this routine up there will not be any Cree's left on the "Eastern Shore", HA! HA! Adam and Hess get in the Kubota and drive on down to the pier.

Chapter 14

EXOSET MISSILE DRIFTWOOD EAGLE

November 29, 2007 Thursday morning back at the AEA in Las Vegas, Nevada. DAE Chief Engineer Cedric Fauntleroy "Nerdy" is in his office reviewing Exoset Missile operational test procedure Programs on his CPU. He and his boss the Exoset Missile Program manager Norman Savage are elated over the programs progress and are working on the final operational test procedures.

Norman calls the front desk. Yes Mr. Savage how may I help you! Betty please call Miss Anna Belle at her work cubicle and tell her to report to Nerdy's office ASAP. Yes, Sir! Anna Belle has been working with Nerdy as his new assistant since early July and shows great interest in the Exoset Missile Program. Anna walks in, Nerdy greets her. As she sits down he tells her upfront that he needs her to help plan and to go on an out of town trip with him to support the Exoset Missile operational test programs. Anna is that a problem, it may require you to be out of town two weeks maybe more? Gosh no Nerdy, I need a break from this damn place. Where are we going, when do we leave and can we stay in the same Hotel room together, HA! HA!? Nerdy gets embarrassed as they all laugh. Norman steps in and states that's a no, no, as it is against company policy. Just kidding boss I just like to tease Nerdy and watch him turn red. You little shit ass!

Anna you will enjoy this company / Uncle Sam paid for trip it is close to your home in Williamsburg, Virginia. You and Nerdy are going to fly to Accomac County, Virginia to support the WISC folks on these planned Prototype Exoset Missile tests. Wonderful, when do we leave? Monday the 3rd of December. Holy Shit that's in four days, hell Nerdy you do not give a girl a chance to do her triple "S". Nerdy laughs and says "I did not know girls shaved." We do but not our faces! Again Nerdy gets embarrassed as they all laugh at his expense once more. Damn he is easy!

Norman says folks let's get serious as a lot of people know and realize this Exoset Missile is now the most lethal weapon in our U.S. Military Arsenal at this time. Many, Enemy Terrorist Groups and other Unfriendly Foreign Powers have agents in place as we speak who will try and get their hands on any part of this missile program that they can.

Anna as you realize nothing we have discussed leaves this room. Everything we have discussed is "TOP SECRET". Yes Sir I understand, I have all the clearances required. Anna we realize this as we reviewed your clearance status before hiring you.

To safely ship a Prototype Exoset Missile we have placed and packed each of the five components that make up the missile assembly in five separate Military Hypergolic Containers that keeps them under a controlled atmospheric condition. Each of the two prototype missile assemblies will be shipped in separate special designed heavy duty wood crates. These crates will be identified with a decal that shows a picture of an American Bald Eagle Head on Driftwood. Code name for shipping and handling of an Exoset Prototype Missile is "DRIFTWOOD EAGLE".

Norman when do you and Nerdy plan on shipping these crated "Driftwood Eagles"? The two prototypes missile crates departed minutes ago, one each on separate aircraft from right here at AEA. First stop Langley Field Air Force Base, Hampton Virginia. Second stop, separate helicopter flights from Langley Field to WISC Complex, Wallops Island, Virginia.

Any more questions! Yes Anna where are we staying over on the Eastern Shore? I have you both reserved lodging at an old popular Inn and Restaurant complex near New Church named the Delmarva Inn. It is located close to the WISC Complex. Great! If no more questions folks that's all I have for now. Nerdy yes! One more thing what time do we depart Monday? Well tomorrow is a full work day, let me confirm your flight again but at this time you will leave Monday morning early right at 0630Hr right from here. That's it, have a safe trip as Norman leaves.

Anna starts to leave, Anna before you leave can I ask you one personal question? Nerdy you can ask me anything you wish sweet heart. If it's a marriage proposal; my answer is yes!!!! Anna laughs! Anna you are a piece of work will you stop that shit you know it embarrasses me. I know Nerdy that's why I do it.

Nerdy what is your question! Why do you wear a glove on your right hand all the time as your left hand is beautiful? Anna gets a serious expression on her face as she begins to weep. Nerdy I injured my right hand severely in a lawnmower accident cutting grass when I was a young girl. I can use my hand somewhat but its ugly to look at especially with one finger missing so I cover it by wearing a glove. I understand I am sorry I ask. That's OK Nerdy better let me get back to work. Fine I will see you tomorrow call if you have any questions.

Meanwhile over at the Secret Peace Corp Earth Base Station (SPCEBS) new agent Dennis Farrel NV36C is in his office working as his CP vibrates (Note: Dennis Farrel is one of the twenty new Secret Peace Corp Trained Agents and now works full time at the SPCEBS). Yes Lieutenant (Lt) Ree what can I do for you this fine day? How do you like your new SPC job? I love it! We'll on the outside continue to keep it Top Secret, you know the rules! Yes Sir Lt no worry I have a private Law Investigating Business working out of my office at home. It is doing great and is an excellent front that covers my SPC Job here at the SPCEBS very well, no worry.

Dennis the reason I called you is to verify that you were able to take care of the Exoset Missile Shipping Crates over at the DAE Complex last night as we discussed? Yes Sir, I drove over parked in the visitor's area. When the coast was clear I put myself into my SPC Demineralized Invisible State (DIS). I walked in to the shipping department at the DAE as they were packing the two Prototype Exoset Missile crates. When they stepped away to take a short break I was able to concealed a SPC Sugar Cube in each crate and watched as they came back closed and sealed the crates, no problems. Great good job Dennis.

Dennis I spoke with our Zone 52 inside agents they confirmed that an al-Qaida Cell may attempt a mission to hijack these crates when and where we do not know at this time. However, we do know at this time where the crates are being shipped. Well Lt Ree we know what to do and anyone tampering with those crates may be in for a huge surprise that's for sure. Thank you Dennis, I will speak with you later, goodbye. Bye Ree!

Meanwhile Don Gear's CPH rings in his new Intelligence (Intel) office in Langley, Virginia. Captain Gear speaking how may I help you? Don it's me Nerdy! Nerdy you old SOB how have you been? Great things could not be any better. You getting any "pusskit" for your dinky? Don you AH you always ask me that.

Nerdy all the feedback news we are getting over here tells us that your Exoset Missile Program is moving along back on schedule and that the fuel, range and guidance problems have been solved, great job ole buddy. Thank you, yes on paper/CPU and 3-DI. Short field test were excellent. Full operational range test are being planned as we speak.

Anyway that is why I called you in the first place. WISC Complex, Wallops Island Virginia on the Eastern Shore of Virginia has won the contract to plan and conduct the remaining full operational Prototype Exoset Missile tests. Nerdy I know; Intell has me assigned to oversee and track this entire program. Well Don I wanted to give you heads up that I will be flying over to the Eastern Shore of Virginia on Monday the 3rd of December to meet with the WISC folks as a DAE consultant on these tests. While I am in town I sure would like to meet up with you and Mela somewhere for supper a couple of nights just to touch base and to see you both.

Damn Nerdy that would be great! Let me check on things and I will get back with you. Mela her twin sister Cela and I all have tons of leave time accumulated. Maybe we can get a few free days leave and drive on over to see you. Good let's plan on it! Have you and Mela set a marriage date yet? No, we have been so busy. That damn Secret Zone 52 bunch she works for is running her and Cela to death and we cannot find the time, just stay loose it will happen. Well Nerdy do not let me hold you any longer. Like I said "I will get right back with you, same CPH number? Yes! Goodbye Nerdy. Goodbye Don.

Chapter 15

VENGEANCE IS MINE

November 29, 2007 Thursday morning. Ring, ring ARMA, Maryrose here how may I help you? Maryrose this is Adam is Allen In his office? Yes he certainly is are you over at the dealership? Yes, just walk on over he is not busy and can see you now. I will be right over.

Good morning Adam what is on your mind? Well I am sitting over there in the office bored to death as car sales are slow and I have too much time to think. When this happens my mind goes back to my two failed missions, Jim Turner and the loss of our MC money. Allen I need to eliminate that low life bastard and get it out of my system, get it off my mind and get our stolen MC money back. I know you keep telling me this. Allen it's bugging the liven shit out of me!

Well Adam I tell you what set up a plan and let's go for it. Get it done and out of the way if that will make you satisfied. Allen I already have a plan in place. Throw it on the table let me hear it! Well here is what I would like to do. Let Hess and me drive over to Middlesex County tomorrow morning early. We drive to Toppers Air Field. Hess unknown to anyone over there goes in to speak with Jim Turner about leasing an Aircraft Hangar. Amy, Jim Turner's secretary will of course send Hess down the hall to Jim's back office. Hess goes back, once inside he forces Jim Turner to open his office safe and return all of the money he stole out of my MC box plus anything else of value, what the hell. Hess then shoots Jim Turner and eliminates the PAS. In the meantime I walk in a short time later shoot and eliminate Amy. Hess and I walk out get in the car and drive back over here. Piece a cake, done deal, no problems. Two worthless infidel POS eliminated! How great is that! Sounds good go for it!

Your plans sounds great to me Adam go for it. It's the only way you are going to get these POS off your back. Adam please remember the one thing Mom use to tell us "always be careful when seeking vengeance. Revenge can reverse itself." "Vengeance is mine"!!!!!

November 30, 2007 Friday morning about 0800Hr a beautiful Cadillac automobile drives from the Eastern Shore over to Middlesex County and pulls off of Rt 3 into the parking area of the Toppers Airport Mangers Building and Office. One man (Hess) gets out of the car. The parking lot is empty except for Jim Turners truck, Amy's car and the airport Kubota.

Amy standing at the office front window is looking out through the slightly opened blinds drinking a cup of coffee and watching the car that just pulled up. The man that just got out of the car is standing still, acting very strange and appears to be very nervous. The man begins walking towards the front door as he gets close he pulls out a small hand gun from his pocket and stops to check it out and look around. Amy runs gets down and hides behind her desk. Amy texts Jim in the back office "heads up Jim we have bad company and trouble coming onboard".

The man enters and hollers "anybody home"! He looks around as if to get some response. He slowly walks down the hallway towards the back office. He hollers once again "anybody home"! This time he clearly has his pistol drawn and pointed as he opens the office door. Jim hears him and like Amy is also hidden on the floor behind his desk, in his hand is his old forty five caliber automatic pistol.

The man (Hess) steps in; Jim shouts whoever you are drop your gun and put up your hands and turn around. The man complies. Jim looks him straight in the eyes and does not blink. Who are you and what the hell do you want? We came to get our money. What money, what the hell are you talking about? The fuckin money you stole out of Adam Rasouls 1941 Packard Hearse last October. BS I have never stolen any money from Adam Rasoul or anyone else in my life.

Jim slowly text Sheriff Jim Wright! "Sheriff get your ass over here to my office PDQ we are being held up and robbed". Sheriff Wright texts a reply right back "I am on the way". Meanwhile up front Adam Rasoul walks in through the front door as planned with his pistol already drawn. Amy still hidden recognizes Adam and now realizes this is a life or death situation and has removed her small thirty eight caliber pistol .from her purse. Amy points the gun straight at Adam. Amy very nervous at this time moves as Adam hears her and looks around. He spots Amy behind and under the desk and fires off two rounds, lucky for Amy both shots miss. Amy returns fire as she squeezes off two rounds of her own. Both rounds strike Adam in his upper body. Adam goes down severely wounded.

The sound of the shots startle Jim and he shakes, turns and drops his guard. Hess sees a chance and jumps Jim and knocks him down. As Jim falls he drops his gun. Hess quickly picks up the gun turns and starts to shoot Jim; bam, bam, two shots ring out as Amy steps in and squeezes off two quick rounds. One shot misses Hess but the second shot hits him cleanly in the back of his head. Hess goes down and the PAS is dead before he even hits the floor.

Jim shaking like a leaf looks at Amy and shouts "my dear you just saved my life that towel head bastard was going to kill me in cold blood." Amy also shaking begins to cry as she and Jim grab and hold each other tightly. Amy why are they here, why would they want to kill us? Jim I do not understand we supported and helped Adam Rasoul and his "Wilson and Wilson Aviation Company" with open arms the two years they leased property from us here at Toppers Field. Why would he do this I thought we were friends! Amy my dear they are al-Qaida Terrorist that's what they do, that's all they know, we are considered infidels fighting against their cause.

After calming themselves down somewhat Amy and Jim hear in the distance the sirens of the Sheriff and another Deputy's car coming this way to their office. As usual lights flashing and sirens blaring just enough to let the whole fuckin County know they are on the way.

Sheriff Jim Wright and the Deputy drive up, jump out and walk in. Amy and Jim meet them at the front door, when the Sheriff sees they are safe he orders the Deputy to go back out and disperse the small crowd that begins to form outside the office building.

The Hartfield Volunteer Fire and Rescue Squad arrive; they exam Adam and Hess the two wounded Towel heads. Both POS of course are dead thanks to Amy's excellent marksmanship! The Rescue Squad folks place the two dead bodies in body bags and transport them up to a local Funeral Home morgue in Saluda to be stored and cared for until fully identified and claimed by family members.

Jim tells Sheriff Jim Wright basically what took place and that he and Amy will give him more details later but for now they are going home just to be alone and settle down. Before they leave Jim calls his standby assistant and tells him to report in and oversee the Airport Operations while he is away. He also calls the Maid Service to come in to clean up and put the office back in working order. Amy still very upset walks over and gets in Jim's truck. Jim tells the Sheriff good bye he too gets in the truck and he and Amy drive on home.

The Sheriff waves good bye and thinks to himself "no wonder Amy is so upset it is not every day that a beautiful lady like Amy Turner gets to kill two towel head POS and save her husband's life".

An afterthought: Like Mom said "be careful, Vengeance is mine said the Lord", TYDL.

Chapter 16

SECRET PEACE CORP TRAINING IS COMPLETE

November 29, 2007 Thursday morning. Good morning my dear little buttercup did you sleep well? Aren't you romantic today, yes I did just like a little baby. What's for breakfast this fine day? Sausage, eggs scrambled with cream cheese and fresh basil; hot buttered grits and hot Black English tea. Shit Susan you cannot buy this breakfast at "BEEJOES" Buffet in Las Vegas.

John finishes eating his breakfast and gets up to go out to the Boat House as his SPC Cell Pad (CP) vibrates. Damn it's JC. What's up JC did you and Atlee have a nice Thanksgiving? Yes, we sure did. On PA we do not celebrate Thanksgiving but here on PE we do. It's a wonderful Holiday Tradition.

Look John what I called you about is to tell you and Susan about our SPCEBS Training Plans and Schedules. Is Susan there? Yes, she is right here. Good click her CP on and you also stay connected. Hi JC how are you? Just fine! How about Atlee? She is fine, sassy as ever. Great!

Susan I wanted to let you know right up front that we are changing our SPC Training Plans and Procedures as follows: First off with only twenty new members we are not planning any on site classes here at the SPCEBS at this time. Shit JC I was looking forward to coming that way and seeing the SPCEBS Complex John has told me so much about it. Do not worry Susan we plan on giving an open house tour in the future to all our agents old and new.

Susan let me continue, since all new members are being trained on the job by their spouses and close friends who are already established SPC Agents we are satisfied that this training will suffice, feedback supports this. Susan what remains to complete your training is for the SPCEBS medical department to meet with you so that they can insert the two "undetectable microchips" in your body that give you access to the two SPC Weapons that they support. Yes JC, John has told me all about them and has demonstrated them for me. Great!

Well Susan here is what we would like to do if it's agreeable with you and John. Atlee works with our Medical Staff here at the SPCEBS and is qualified to insert these Microchips. We would like to Air Tram (AT) over to your place tomorrow Friday the 30ᵗʰ if you are available and have Atlee perform the procedures and insert these microchips in your body. Is that OK? No problem John and I will be right here fly on over and drop in! One question does it hurt I have a very low tolerance for pain, HA! HA! No Susan not at all; as a matter of fact our new insertion procedures will overwhelm you it is so quick, simple and painless. It may take Atlee a second or two to insert both Microchips that's about all. Good! Atlee and I will see you both about 0900Hr tomorrow morning. Thank you JC have a safe trip good bye!

Well my dear the beat goes on! Yes I know but I was sure looking forward to another trip to Las Vegas to see Atlee's and JC cottage and tour the SPCEBS. Do not be disappointed my dear it will come to pass as JC said "they are planning a future SPCEBS open house and tour". At least after tomorrow you will have for the most part all of your SPC Training complete and behind you, TYDL. I just had a great idea, its 1200Hr and a beautiful day let's go out and sit on the pier drink beer and watch the gulls squawk, fly around and shit. Wonderful idea let's go!

November 30, 2007 Friday morning about 0900Hr. John's CP vibrates, it's JC, he and Atlee are right on time as usual. Hello JC where are you? We are 50K feet straight above your house, is the coast clear? Yes sir, drop your AT down to the usual area and park it in the barn as before; no one here but Susan and I and the front gate is locked.

Susan and John watch as JC lands the AT, what a way to travel. Atlee and JC walk up as Susan and John gives them both a big hug. Come on in coffee and fresh biscuits are hot and on the table. Great Susan your fresh biscuits are to die for.

After eating and chatting for a while JC says "let's get down to the business of why we came over here in the first place". Susan are you ready? No but let's get it over with. Good, time is short and I also have a mission Lt Ree gave me just before we left that just came up I want to discuss with you both.

Oh! By the way while we were hovering overhead we noticed in the direction of your small airfield a crowd was gathering and a lot of flashing red, blue and yellow lights. Something has happened over there; may be a plane accident of some kind! Damn JC we have not looked at any news this morning on TV and I have not turned our scanner on in the boat house or in here. I will have to check it out later.

Atlee I understand you are going to insert my two SPC Microchips. Is this something we need to do in the bedroom where I need to lie down? Atlee just laughs, no Susan I can conduct these procedures right here in front of John and JC: no worry, no problems. Atlee opens her CP. John and Susan are puzzled. Atlee looks at their expressions and grins. Susan this this is the latest procedure developed recently by our PA Medical Laboratory Research Team.

Atlee removes two minute very small pill shaped containers from her CP. She also takes out a packet that contains a latex looking fingertip sleeve. Susan lay your left hand on the table palm up and be very still. Atlee presses on the small container it breaks open and a small drop of white glowing cream oozes out. She picks this up with her latex covered fingertip and gently presses it into Susan's left palm. Done, did that hurt? Hurt hell you have not done anything yet! Susan I just inserted one of your Microchips. No way, no needles! Susan on PA we use needles for needle point or other art work and hobbies as they all laugh.

Susan in a few seconds you should feel a slight tingle in your forehead. I feel it now. Wonderful, procedure over and complete! Susan you now have the SPC Weapon at your disposal to eliminate anyone via a silent heart attack just by touching their neck area. WOW, God help us!!!!

Susan when using this weapon you can think "heart attack" or "faint attack". Faint attack of course just puts the victim down in a mild sleep that will not kill them. Susan here is the very serious part related to this Microchip. If for any reason you become hostile and stray from your SPC duties the SPCEBS and the SPCB on PA have the ability to eliminate you in seconds via a similar silent heart attack. I know John explained this to me very clearly. JC interrupts: much to my sadness this happens. John you may be surprised but two members of your SPC graduating class have been removed via this method. Some folks get carried away with the power they have using our SPC Weapons and they lose control. So sad!

Susan let's get started and insert your second Microchip. The same procedure applies except I apply the cream from the second container under your left arm pit area as you are right handed. This is done, no problem. Susan both Microchips have now been inserted successfully in your body simply by rubbing the proper cream into your skin. What do you think, how great is that! What s breakthrough for medical science on PA, hopefully your medical folks here on PE will follow and develop these procedures in the future. Atlee it's unbelievable. Susan you can now after your forehead tingling subsides put yourself into a SPC Demineralized Invisible State (DIS), how great is that. Has the tingling stopped? Yes! Hell let's give it a shot and see what happens.

Susan stands up very nervous as expected. She reaches under her left arm close to where Atlee rubbed the cream. Instantly she completely disappears. Holy Shit what a SPC weapon! Thank the Good Lord we have this weapon at our disposal and not the Terrorist. Susan repeats the procedure and instantly reappears, she delighted. They all give her a big hug as her SPC Training for now is complete. JC tells her "Susan you now have under your complete control all of our SPC PA Secret Weapons; CP, Silent Invisible Laser, Sugar Cubes, Silent Heart Attack and DIS. Please train and learn how to use and control all five to the best of your ability. Use them and help us to continue to promote Peace Here on PE and throughout the Universe as the Good Lord has requested this is our primary mission, TYDL.

JC says folks "with our new SPC Agent VA10C Training now complete I have a Mission I need to discuss with you both that may be developing in your area over on the "Eastern Shore". As JC continues he is interrupted as John's CP vibrates. Hello, yes Jim, Jim you sound excited. Jim calm down and wait just a minute if you will, thank you!!!! JC its Jim Turner the Topper's Airport Field Manager. John go ahead and complete your call I am not in any hurry.

Folks, all of you need to listen up to this call as John clicks on the CP remote speaker system! Go ahead Jim. John have you heard the news?

What news, Susan and I have been so busy we have not turned on our Television Sets (TV) or Scanners today what news? Well you are not going to believe this. Our good friend form Wilson Aviation, Adam Rasoul and another terrorist thug showed up at my office early this morning. John they drove up parked and barged right in. John it was terrifying for me and my dear Amy; what an experience. The thug with Adam came at me with a gun and demanded I return money I stole from a MC Adam had hidden in his old 1941 Packard Hearse. John I do not know what money the bastard was talking about but I know they were here to rob us get that MC money back and I am sure to murder Amy and I before they left. John that PAS Adam Rasoul was going to murder us both in cold blood!!!!! Can you believe that!

Jim how in the world were you able to stop the attack, what happened? John would you believe my little Amy shot and killed both of those POS! SOB Jim are you kidding me? Are you and Amy OK! John we are doing better now that we are at home resting but it will take a few days to get over the trauma. Amy is taking it very hard. I can understand that.

John I realize I am holding you up but the main reason I called is to give you heads up. I know you did a lot of routine investigating over in that Hangar "A" when we leased it to Adam Rasoul so if you can think of anything that may support Sheriff Wrights investigation I know he would appreciate your help. Jim thank you for calling! I will call Sheriff Wright and speak with him later. Jim tell Amy hello and thank God for her marksmanship. Go sip a cold one get some rest and if you and Amy need anything please call us. Good bye!

Well folks how about that! JC that was the disturbance you guys witnesses over at the Airport early this morning just before you landed. What do you think! Where did those two POS come from, it has to be close by for them to have come by car. JC I think we know about the missing MC money they were looking for. I removed that money from Adam's 1941 Packard Hearse just before we let him and Javid depart Toppers Airfield Field on Halloween Night October 31st. Damn poor Jim Turner and Amy almost took the rap for something I did. Thank God Amy was able to take them out first, TYDL.

John let me get back to this mission I would like to discuss with you, after hearing Mr. Turners phone call it may be related to what took place this morning over at Toppers Airport. JC go ahead but I am like you I have a hunch you may be right about that they may be related.

JC continues, folks I will keep it short; information we have just received from our two SPC Agents working undercover inside the local secret Zone 52 office tell us a very small al-Qaida Cell located on the Eastern Shore of Virginia is beginning to expand and become a very active player. What I would like to do John is have you and our new agent VA10C sitting here investigate this Cell. It may not be much to it but you never know. JC does this al-Qaida Cell have a code name? Right now it is called "The Delly Rode Cell". We suspect its leader to be a man named Allen Rasoul.

Hell JC there is your connection. Hell, that AH Amy Turner shot and killed this morning is Allen Rasoul's brother. Adam is the AH that set up and planned the Newport Ship & Dock Company and The Defense Destroy Guided Missile Ship DDG-911 missions that we just completed. Hell JC that is where the PAS hauled ass to on October 31st when he departed Toppers Field. John you are on top of this you got it! You and Susan take over! No problem, no worry JC, VA10A and VA10C will take over and handle "The Delly Rode" al-Qaida Cell investigation and mission. Thank you Susan and John now let's go out to the Boat House and drink a cold beer its 1200Hr somewhere. SOB JC you are beginning to turn into a bad ass red neck. I know Atlee has been telling that too! They all laugh!

Well if you guys are finally finished talking about your mission I have one more thing I need to do before we go out to the boat house. What is that Atlee? I need to complete my medical procedures? Hell we thought you were finished. I need to clean up this trash and dispose of it properly. Hell Atlee it's just a couple of small containers and a latex fingertip sleeve just throw it all in that trash can in the corner. I know Susan but it is all made out of special Chargren materials from PA. Atlee gathers it all up, takes it outside, puts it on the ground, takes out her CP and zaps the small pile of debris with her SPC laser. It all vaporizes, nothing remains. All done let's go get that cold beer my medical duties for today are complete! JC looks at her, well done my dear your SPC training has served you well.

Chapter 17

THE DELLY RODE MISSION BEGINS

December 01,2007 Saturday morning. John is up early. John for heaven's sake what has gotten into you and where are you going this early? Susan my dear I just thought of a clue that may give us a lead on that Delly Rode al-Qaida Terrorist Cell. Damn your hunches, clues and that SPC is going to kill you can't it wait? No I need to run over to Toppers Field Airport and check it out before Sheriff Wrights Depos come and remove all the evidence from yesterday's crime scene. Hon, just sleep in I will be back shortly and we can have a late breakfast together. Fine with me just be careful, I love you. I love you too!

John quickly drives over to Toppers Field and pulls into the office building parking area. Much to his surprise Jim Turners truck is parked out front. He goes on in and shouts for Jim. John I am back here come on back! What the hell are you doing over here this early as he gives Jim a big hug? They have been lifelong friends forever. Hell John I could not sleep and just felt like I needed to come over here and check things out. John what are you doing over here?

Hell Jim you know me playing cops and robbers. Shit John it's in your blood what's on your mind? Well when you called yesterday I thought of a few things I might be able to pass on to Sheriff Wright that may be related to this robbery attempt of yours. Let's go outside I need to check on something. Speaking of the Devil here comes Sheriff Jim Wright now.

Sheriff Wright pulls in. Good morning John and Jim I did not expect to see you two guys standing out here. Good morning Sheriff I drove over to check out a few things plus I might have a couple things I know about Adam Rasoul that may help your investigation. John you old rascal crime scene work is in your blood, they all laugh. Great John what have you got for me?

Sheriff no longer being on the force is it OK if I ask you and Jim some questions? Yes by all means, John I can always use your help you know that just keep it between us. First what type of vehicle did they drive up in? John it's that's beautiful new 2007 Cadillac, parked over there. That's why I am here I came over to take care of the car and get it returned back to its rightful owners. Hell Adam Rasoul and the other thug we now know as "Hess" stole the car from a dealership over on the Eastern Shore. BS Sheriff I do not believe that for one minute. Well John here is what I have found out so far and it checks out.

John I verified that the VIN found on the car is registered to a used car Dealership on the Eastern Shore located near "New Church". The name of the dealership is "Dewey Duzz Do Cars"! Hell Sheriff the metal frame around the license plate on the car trunk tells you that. Well I looked the dealership up on the CPU and called them. John I will admit this is where it does get somewhat strange. A very nice lady answered the phone and identified herself as Dayzee Duzz. I told her who I was and that my office has impounded a car that is registered to them. The phone went silent then she came back on and mumbled a few words of some kind. Then all of a sudden she asks a stupid question. "What car is that?" I told her all about the car!

John she then changed her tone of voice and went on to explain that two strange looking men had been in several times to look at that car and that last Thursday they came back to test drive it one more time. She told me she did a foolish thing, she was so busy she let them take the car out for a test drive and did not go with them, talk about stupid. Anyway to make a long story short they did not bring the car back and of course you know the rest of the story.

Now John this is where her story really gets strange. She ask me did I catch and arrest the two thugs that stole her car as she would like to call and speak with them if possible? Why do you suppose she would want to do something like that? I have never heard of such a thing.

I told her that the two thugs attempted to rob the Toppers Field Airport manager and both were killed in a shootout. John I am not sure but I think she dropped the phone. After a long pause she got back on the phone and I could tell she had been crying. I ask her if she was all right? She said "no problem she was fine". She told me she would send someone over here early today to pick up the car. I gave her this location. She said "thank you" and hung up. John what do you think? Sheriff you know what I think!!!!!!!!!! BS, BS and more BS! If it looks like a duck, quacks like a duck; Jim it's a fuckin duck you know that! Sheriff I rode over this morning to check out this car as I just had a hunch it may have come from the Eastern Shore area. Anyway one of the things I was going to tell you is I believe this entire story is going to expand and unravel on the Eastern Shore of Virginia and this car now supports that. John you may be right but my investigation work over here in Middlesex County on this case is complete.

Jim being that you are here will you take this envelope and give it to Amy for me! By the way how is she doing, better I hope? Yes she is better but the trauma yesterday has taken a lot out of her, thanks for asking. Jim I can just imagine that! I told her to just stay home a few days and just rest. Sheriff her bucket list has a lot of things on it but killing two terrorist POS was not one of them. Well tell her I said "hello and just forget about it." Jim she did all of us a big favor. Middlesex County owes her a great debt of gratitude and I am very proud of her. Thank you Sheriff!

Well fellows let me run I have got things I need to take care of and waiting around here all day is not one of them. Jim if and when the folks from over on the Eastern Shore arrive to pick up this car give me a call? Will do! Sheriff one thing before you go this envelope is sealed; as Amy's husband can I open it? Yes Jim you can, go ahead it contains all the legal paperwork exonerating Amy of any wrong doing: and that her actions yesterday were based on human self-defense as reviewed by the Commonwealth's Attorney Office and considered Justifiable Homicide. Damn Sheriff this is great news as this is all that is on her mind; "what are they going to do to me"? Jim you tell her nothing but pin a metal on her. They all laugh as Sheriff Jim Wright drives off. Jim I need to run also is there anything you or Amy need? No John, nothing I can think of "Just Time to Heal" TYDL.

Back home Susan is up as John walks in. Well "Dick Tracy" did you find and get the information you drove over there for? Yes my dear little butter cup. I found what I was looking for and much more. Let's eat breakfast and I will run it all by you as we eat. Great, how do you want your eggs? Scrambled with cream cheese and fresh basil! Coming up my dear!

Chapter 18

A TRIP TO DELMARVA

December 01, 2007 late Saturday morning. Well my dear how was that breakfast? Outstanding! Susan on a more serious note you can see by the conversation we just completed over breakfast and what I just told you about Amy and Jim Turner's ordeal that this al-Qaida bunch are terrorist thugs and cold blooded killers. I know John and it terrifies me to think people can be that cruel. Why? Why? We all have so much Dear God why can't we just live in Peace?

Well here are the plans I feel we need to put in place at this time. Susan jump in with your suggestions at any time. John my dear before you start; I can tell you this we need to get over to the Delmarva Peninsula, now like PDQ. My dear Susan spoken like a true SPC Agent! VA10C welcome aboard!

Well let's lay out a few plans and arrange on leaving Monday morning the 3rd of December. Great I will check the CPU go online and get us reservations for a Hotel, close to the Wallops Island Space Center Complex (WISC), if we get a chance we can ride over and tour the WISC Complex who knows. How many days are we looking at John? Hell, let's say four at least; let's make it a short vacation trip. While you are working on that I think I will call Lt Ree at the SPCEBS and get all the latest facts on this Delly Rode Cell bunch he may have received since JC spoke with him.

Lt Ree's CP at the SPCEBS vibrates. Yes VA10A what's on your mind? Lt Ree JC assigned "The Delly Rode Mission to Susan and me. Yes John I know this! Well fill me in on what you know so far about this bunch of thugs. I cannot do this John you need to speak with Agent NV36C he is my right hand man and he controls the file on that Mission. You know the new guy Dennis Farrel? Lt Ree you AH if you are trying to be funny, do not quit your day job, HA! HA! Ree how is he doing? Great, a workaholic and a very sharp law man and investigator. I told you so! Ree click me over to him? Will do, have a nice day John, tell Susan hello.

VA10A, John you old bastard how are you and what can I do for you this fine day? I am doing great how about yourself? John if it gets any better I do not think I could stand it. Glad to hear that. Dennis I will not hold you long as I know you are busy but I am sure you know JC assigned the Delly Rode Cell mission to Susan and me. Yes I just found out, hell its right in your backyard. Well fill me in on any facts you know related this Mission. John I was going to call you and go over this but to be honest there is not much I can tell you but here is what I have compiled so far.

The DAE shipped out two Prototype Exoset Missiles Code name "Driftwood Eagle" in separate crates to the WISC Complex, Wallops Island Virginia. John these shipping crates each have decals attached showing a picture of a carved American Bald Eagle Head on Driftwood if you locate these crates look for those decals. Our SPC Agents working inside of Zone 52 tipped us off that an al-Qaida Cell may attempt to hijack at least one of these crates. That said, Lt Ree had me drive over to the DAE Company shipping warehouse and place a SPC sugar cube in each crate should they get hijacked. John that way we / you can at least find and destroy the missile components with our SPC CP Invisible Laser taking the missile away from them. Hell if we cannot get the missile crate back on our own it's better to destroy it than letting them succeed.

Anyway John that's all the information I have at this time. Oh, one more thing and I will let you go. The DAE gentleman in charge is a DAE Chief Engineer whose name is Cedric Fauntleroy a. k. a. "Nerdy". They say he is a genius when it comes to Aerospace Technology of any kind. A regular Albert Einstein / Von Braun all rolled into one! Dennis one thing I would like to know is how can the al-Qaida people know about any of these missile shipments? John we are not sure but we think they may be receiving inside information from Fauntleroy's young assistant Anna Belle; we are investigating this as we speak. She, Savage and Fauntleroy are the only inside persons aware of these "Driftwood Eagle" Shipments. Dennis before I go how is that beautiful Desiree Watts of yours doing? John that beautiful creature sits on my face every night. Dennis you AH, good bye!

December 03, 2007 Monday morning early before sunrise Susan and John are up getting ready to leave for the Delmarva Peninsula! All packed with reservations confirmed at the Delmarva Inn located in the New Church area they get in their old Ford F-150 truck and depart.

They drive as John likes to call it the "Big Loop": over, up and around through Virginia Beach, back down and on across the CBBT System to the Eastern Shore. Heading north towards Kiptopeke John begins to think about the old days. He says to Susan do you realize the last time I was over this way had to be thirty or thirty five years ago. Our old neighbors; Pellam Green, Phil Wessel's, Melvin Cobb and I trailered our old Wellcraft boat over to the town of "Oyster" to flounder fish.

Susan what I remember the most about that trip is stopping at the Cape Charles Truck Stop Restaurant just up here on the right. Would you believe that damn Pellam got a live minnow from the live bait bucket and took it inside with him? We all ordered breakfast and he put that damn live minnow in his water glass after the waitress finished filling it. When she returned with our orders he ask her what that was swimming around in his glass. Pellam expecting a loud scream or at least some panic. All he got was a stern look from the waitress as she said "it's a bull minnow AH we use them over here all the time to catch flounder; what the fuck did you think it was"? Pellam looked up and just grinned! SOB, Phil, Mel and I went down for the fuckin count; damn that was funny! Damn Susan, those were some wonderful days long gone; where does the time go? Don't blink your eyes my dear, just thank the good Lord for each and every day!!!!

John and Susan drive up to the entrance of the Delmarva Inn they stop and go inside to check in. Just in front of them is a young couple also checking in. After the young couple have completed checking in John and Susan step up to the front counter. Yes folks glad to have you stop by how may I help you?

John and Susan James we just arrived! Yes sir Mr. and Mrs. John James I have you listed right here, Room Number 3 ground floor level front. Great son no stairs to climb, we are not young newlyweds like the couple that just signed in. The clerk just laughed, Mr. James they are not newlyweds either. That was Mr. Fauntleroy and his assistant Anna Belle from DAE in town from Las Vegas. They are your neighbors he has Room No.1 and she has Room No.2 next to you guy's. John just mumbles, oh, how nice!

As he and Susan walk away John tells her that young man was Cedric Fauntleroy the Chief Engineer from DAE Dennis told us about. Damn John he looks like he is about twelve years old. I know and a nerd at that. That beautiful young lady with him is Anna Belle. She is his assistant at DAE and is the suspected al-Qaida Spy the SPC and Zone 52 are investigating to verify. Damn John how does a young beautiful girl like that get herself involved in terrorist activities? Hon I will never know, it beats me; like the man said "you can't fix stupid" Susan I guess we sort of lucked out at least we now know what those two folks look like and who to look for if need be.

Maryrose's phone rings, hello ARMA how may I help you? Maryrose this is Anna Belle is Doctor Allen Rasoul in his office? Yes he certainly is just a minute please, Doc it's for you! Hello! Doc it's me Anna Belle I am here in town over at the Delmarva Inn right across the road from you. Me and Nerdy just checked in. I have a nice package here for you. Wonderful I have been checking the Exmore Post Office daily for something from you. Sorry about that Doc I should have texted you. Nerdy invited me on this trip as his assistant to meet with the WISC Complex folks plus he knew it was close to my Williamsburg home town, nice guy. Anyway I was able to conceal the package and bring it along instead of mailing it to you. Great, can you get free and bring it over? Yes sir I think so, no problem. By the way Dayzee is sitting right here and she is also anxious to see you again. Wonderful I am on my way over.

Dayzee that was Anna Belle she is over at the Delmarva Inn and she is on the way over can you stay a while longer? Yes Allen but I am still very upset. I know me too! Anna Belle walks in and Maryrose takes her right in to Doc's office. She gives Doc and Dayzee a big hug as she has not seen them in years. She can tell by looking at them both they are very upset about something. Folks you both look upset am I interrupting something? No not really as we can tell you as we have always considered you family since you came onboard as one of our most trusted al-Qaida agents.

Anna we have just recently received some very bad news! Our beloved brother Adam and my trusted assistant Hess were both killed in a tragic accident early last Friday morning. "Praise be to Allah"! How did that happen? Anna it's a long story we can discuss at another time. Allen let me go I know you and Anna have serious al-Qaida business to discuss. OK, sis take care of yourself we will get through this, time heals all wounds. Bye Anna nice to see you again! Thank you Dayzee, nice to see you! Damn Doc Dayzee is a wreck! I know, we lost Abraham, now Adam so she is worried to death something will happen to me. Hell Anna I am the only close family member she has left.

Anna what do you have for me? Anna opens her carry on air flight bag. Doc I believe you will be very pleased with what I have for you, anyway I certainly hope so. She takes out and opens a small eight" x ten" inch box. It contains CD Crystals of the complete Exoset Missile Prototype Assembly Package code name "Driftwood Eagle". Doc I also was able to get the 3D-I of the Special Designed Shipping crates you requested plus six copies of the shipping crate secret "Driftwood Eagle" decals. SOB Anna, terrific work I sure did not expect to receive all off this information; Rahism Badhdadi is going to be very pleased with you to say the least. "Praise be to Allah"! Anna I do not know how you did it but again great job! She just laughs, Doc letting young bucks have a little pie at the "Y" every now and then will go a long way and get you everything, HA! HA! You little bitch you know I love you!!!!! Anna just smiles!

Anna how long are you and "Nerdy" as you call him planning on staying in town? Doc I am not really sure! He has given me the green light to go and play and do what I want too. I do know he has meetings scheduled for the next few days with the WISC folks to discuss the Prototype Exoset Missile Assemblies and Operational Tests. Nothing that will involve me.

Well Doc let me leave and get on back across the road. Thank you again Anna you have done our cause a great service and like I said "Rashism Badhdadi will be very pleased." I hope so! Anna I will call you when we have meetings at the Cedar View Farm. As you may remember I try to keep all of our Delly Rode Cell activity completely separate from my ARMA School business. I remember that, I guess I should have held the package for later but I was so excited to bring it to you I could not wait. That's fine dear every now and then things like this just happen.

Go now and keep a low profile. As she leaves she gives Doc a big hug and say's "I am so sorry about the loss of your dear brother Adam. Thank you Anna! Doc by the way if you should need me I am in Room No.2, Nerdy is in Room No.1. Good Bye I will talk with you later!

Chapter 19

INVESTIGATION TIME

December 03, 2007 Monday afternoon. Baka's CPH at the Cedar View Farm rings! Hello Baka here! Baka this is Doc listen up this is what I want you to do. Go by yourself to the Barn Magazine Storage Area. Take those six large boxes of High Yield Dynamite Round Sticks we have stored there load them up in an ARMA School truck and bring them up to Dewey's Junk Yard Chop Shop. You know, the big brick building located far in the back of his lot. Be careful so as not to get stopped by the VASP. I will meet you at Dewey's Chop Shop. No problem Doc I am on my way. I will see you in about an hour.

Doc before I hang up I just want you to know that I am real sorry to hear about the loss of your dear brother Adam and of course our true dear friend Hess. Well thank you Baka I appreciate that. By the way you are now my right hand man replacing Hess. Thank you Doc, big shoes to fill but I will do my best. I will work hard to support you and our cause. Praise be to Allah! Good bye!

Dewey's CPH rings. Dewey here! Dewey this is Doc meet me at your Chop Shop I have a job I need you to take care of PDQ. Doc I am very busy right at the moment can we do it another time? Dewey this is some very serious al-Qaida business; I finally got the Prototype Exoset Missile Package from Anna Belle I was telling you about. Holy Shit Doc I will be right over there.

Doc and Dewey meet at Dewey's Junk Yard Chop Shop just as Baka drives up. Dewey opens the Chop Shop doors and motions to Baka to drive right in and park.

Hi Dewey I have not seen you in quite a spell how have you been? Just fine Baka how about yourself? I have been doing great except Doc is working my fuckin ass off. They all laugh as Doc says "you two get used to it; it's going to get a lot worse the next few weeks that for damn sure".

Doc brings out the package he just received from Anna Belle. Here look at these 3-DI CPU CD. Dewey inserts the CD in his CPU. SOB Doc they are perfect. Dewey can you build and duplicate a wooden crate just like the one shown on this screen? Shit Doc using those 3-DI pictures I can detail and build you a crate to the level no one could ever tell it from the original. The duplication will be a perfect match! Dewey how soon can you build and get me just one finished crate? Doc if I start work now and work on it all night I should complete it and have it ready for you tomorrow morning early. Great Dewey you are a genius!!!!

Dewey here is what I want you to do after you complete the finished crate! Pack it up tightly and carefully using all six boxes of these High Yield Dynamite Round Sticks Baka just brought in from the Farm Magazine. SOB Doc that's one hundred and forty four sticks of High Yield Dynamite; that's enough explosive force to blow the Wallops Island Complex off the fuckin map! Dewey I certainly hope so what a victory for the cause, Praise be to Allah!!!

Dewey before you finish packing the wooden crate solder connect these two detonating cap wires with these pulsating wires to two brass stud bolts protruding through the front of the crate. Attach the wooden crate lifting handles using these same studs in lieu of the usual countersunk wood screws to conceal them. Electrical tape the caps to one of the dynamite sticks. No problem considers it a done deal. Dewey one last thing; take two of these "Driftwood Eagle" decals out of this envelope and paste them upside down one on the front of the crate and one on the back of the completed sealed crate. Note Dewey: "Upside Down"! No worry Doc. When the crate is finished and the job is complete and ready for pick up, Dewey you call me I do not care what time it is, just call me!!! I got you Doc! I got you! Now get the fuck out of here and let me get started you are holding me up and getting on my damn nerves as he pushes Doc and Baka towards the door. Go, go, go just get out of here!!!!!

Doc are you going to ride back to the Farm with me? No Baka, Maryrose and I are going over to pick up Dayzee later and have a little celebration supper and lift a few to honor our wonderful departed brother Adam and our dear friend Hess. Two great men that fought hard for the cause, Praise be to Allah!

Meanwhile over at the Delmarva Inn John says to Susan "are you ready to go out and eat lunch"! No John let's just pass on lunch and eat a big buffet supper at the Delmarva Inn restaurant later tonight. Sounds good to me! If that's the case let's start our investigation into this mission and go snooping and just see if this Delly Rode al-Qaida Cell actually exists and what these fuckin towel head bastards may be up too.

Just before they leave their room John and Susan put themselves into their SPC Demineralized Invisible State (DIS). Susan let's start over at the ARMA School house the Director is Allen Rasoul and he may be the leader of this Delly Rode Cell and it's just across the road.

Susan and John walk across the road to the ARMA School house. Being in their SPC DIS they walk in like they own the place. They see Maryrose at her desk they pass by and walk on in to Allen Rasoul's office. The sign on his desk reads "Dr. Allen Rasoul Director ARMA" a.k.a. "Doc". John whispers to Susan remember he is the suspected "Delly Rode Cell al-Qaida leader. I know a.k.a. "Doc" he must be quite a guy! They continue down the old narrow school hallways every now and then glancing into the old classrooms. Nothing unusual except the sights and smells that bring back old childhood memories from their Old Parkview Elementary School days in Old Warwick County, Virginia. They check the storage area and it also reveals nothing.

Shit Susan this is a waste of time let's go back to the room and put ourselves back into a human state and take a ride over the WISC Complex on Wallops Island and look around and at least locate those "Driftwood Eagle" crates. We still have plenty of time and some daylight remaining!

On the way out of the Delmarva Inn Lobby they run right in to Anna Belle and some guy they have not seen before. Anna nods to them and says Hi. They both nod back and John whispers to Susan "he sure is a sleazy looking bastard she can do better than that." John maybe his good points are concealed in that large bulge in his pants. John laughs is that all you

"Red Neck" girls think about is "Hard Dicks"? HA! HA! Turnabout is fair play my dear.

They drive over to the WISC Complex and pull into the visitor's area parking lot and park. Hell Susan what time is it? Its 1600Hr the sign says 1200Hr-1700Hr for visitors. We are OK! Then they both laugh out loud what the fuck are we concerned about we are going to be in our SPC DIS and can do whatever we please the hell with the time.

John looks around, Susan the coast is clear as they both put themselves back into their SPC DIS. They walk in the main lobby, the place is beautiful. They stop and look at the "Wall Display Directory & Layout Map". Damn Susan I am almost sixty one years old and would you look at how far it is over to the Main Storage Warehouse? John quit your bitchin you are not that old that you can't make it over there and back; besides the walk will do us both good.

They walk over to the Main Warehouse and walk in. Holy Shit this place is huge. Over on the far side sits a test drone the size of a 747 Airliner, it's labeled "Super XPDJP". As they continue to walk and snoop around they come across some tightly closed Black Curtains marked Bay 10 "Driftwood Eagle". They hear voices and slowly squeeze through the curtains. There stands the DAE Chief Engineer Cedric (Nerdy) Fauntleroy going over a few details with the WISC Director Charles Nutmaker. John looks around to establish his position and the Bay 10 exact location. Susan walks around the two Prototype Exoset Missile Shipping crates and checks them out. Charles Nutmaker and Nerdy leave! Susan continues to look around.

Susan always on the lookout for beautiful art work becomes very attracted to the "Driftwood Eagle" Decals. She whispers to John "these Decals are beautiful I sure would like to have one to take home and frame". John laughs; as she tells him "don't laugh John just look at them they are beautiful; a beautiful picture of a American Bald Eagle's Head caved and mounted on a piece of driftwood streamlined to form it's body, how unique is that"? Susie I agree with you my dear but we are here on a serious SPC mission; Susan this is not a trip to a fuckin Waterfowl Art Show!

Susan do you see anything unusual or out of place? No not really! Me neither; let's head on back to the Delmarva Inn drink a couple beers and go eat supper I have found what we came for and I am satisfied that the two Prototype Exoset Missiles (Code Name Driftwood Eagle) arrived safely at the WISC Complex as scheduled and did not get Hijacked by anyone. Shit let's get out of here I am satisfied!!

Back at the Delmarva Inn John tells Susan "so far we have investigated two key suspected area's: the ARMA School Building and the WISC Complex and we have not discovered a damn thing that identifies a major al-Qaida Cell may be operating in this region of Virginia. "Me thinks" someone in Zone 52 may be blowing smoke up Lt Ree's ass! May be so, maybe so; let's go eat supper I am starved!

Chapter 20

THE DRIFTWOOD EAGLE EXCHANGE

December 04, 2007 Tuesday morning very early. Allen Rasoul's CPH rings at his Cedar View Farm. Hello who is the stupid SOB that is calling me at this hour; it's 0400Hr in the damn morning? Doc you AH, the stupid SOB calling you is me; Dewey! You told me to call you when I had the duplicate Prototype Exoset Missile Crate completed regardless of the time of day. Dewey I know, I know! Well you ornery old fuckin bastard your duplicate crate is complete with the High Yield Dynamite Round Sticks installed as discussed. Doc it is a perfect Designed Dynamite Bomb ready to be set off. I just want you to know I have been working my fuckin ass off all night out here in my Chop Shop alone to complete this job for you!!!! Dewey I appreciate that and I apologize for being so rude when I picked up the phone. That's better and more like it. Doc you sure can be a AH at times you know that! I know!

Dewey here is what I am going to do! I am going to call Baka and Nanki and have them drive up to your shop and pick up the completed Duplicated Crate right now. I will have them follow me up and we can review my plans with you and them at the same time. We should be there in about an hour. Fine, Dayzee brought me a big pot of fresh coffee earlier

I will warm it up for us. On your way up stop by Mickey Dee's and pick up some sausage biscuits. Doc I am tired, hungry and I am not in the mood for a lot of BS from you or anyone else!!!! I understand Dewey I know you are tired, just calm down we are on the way!

Baka's CPH rings! Hello, Doc is that you? Yes! Damn Doc do you know what time it is? Yes I sure do! Baka call Nanki meet me out front I want you guys to follow me up to Dewey's he has the duplicated Prototype Exoset Missile crate completed already. Damn that old Cowboy Dewey is a go getter, he does not fuck around that's for sure. Baka drive the big Ford F-250, the one with the full rear shell. Fine Doc we will meet you out front in a few minutes.

Good morning Doc! Good morning Baka, you and Nanki all set? Yes sir! They follow Doc up to Dewey's when Doc arrives he pulls in to Dewey's side driveway and drives all the way to the back and parks near the Chop Shop. Baka follows and sees that Dewey has the Chop Shop doors open so he drives straight in the shop and parks.

Doc gets out of his bright red, brand new Ford F-150 Club Cab truck (Complements of Buddy and Elsa Cree and VIN and title paper work by sister Dayzee). They all greet Dewey look at the duplicate crate and praise him for a job well done. Doc reaches in his truck and takes out a large bag of Mickey Dee's hot sausage biscuits. All four of them sit down, chat, eat breakfast laugh, and wish each other as a joke "Happy Hanukkah" as they pretend the sausage is fish (They should be so lucky. To be of the Jewish religion is a wonderful honor and experience).

Doc goes over all the plans and final details as they load the Duplicate crate on the Ford F-250 truck. He then tells Baka to drive slowly up to the WISC Complex and pull up to the Main Front Gate. Baka if you have any problems ask the Security Officer on duty to telephone the Main Storage Warehouse Manager at CPH Number WH 804. The manager will know what to tell him. Take your time so as not to get pulled over by the VASP. The Warehouse manager is one of our al-Qaida trusted Agents inside just follow his instructions. Just pull into the warehouse and exchange your crate for one of the crates already setting there the manager will help you. When you complete the exchange and leave the WISC Complex drive straight to my Cedar View Farm go directly down to our piers and you and Nanki load the "Driftwood Eagle" Crate onto the "Elsa Cree". Stow it in the hold well below main deck and cover it tightly with the waterproof tarp I have provided. JOB DONE, "COMPLETE"! Go now, be safe, drive safe, Allah be with you.

Dewey my plans for you! Go home get some rest you sure earned it this day. Thanks again for a job well done. Rahism Badhdadi will certainly hear about your work here for our great cause and I know he will be pleased, Praise be to Allah!

Doc follows Baka and Nanki out to the main road, Rt 13. Baka pulls out and turns north heading for the WISC Complex, Doc just cuts across and parks at The ARMA School House and goes on in to his office to put more al-Qaida plans in place.

Over at the Delmarva Inn John is up early as he cannot sleep. Even though he and Susan have not discovered any clues indicating a terrorist Cell may exist he has a hunch they are on track to something but he cannot quite put his finger on it. Being restless he walks over to the front window stirs out and watches the traffic drive by on State Rt 13. He spots the Red Ford F-150 truck coming out of Dewey's side driveway and cutting across Dewey's junk yard parking lot. He watches as it goes over and parks at the ARMA School House. He recognizes the truck and also remembers it being parked over at the ARMA School House yesterday. He also sees the Ford F-250 as it pulls out and turns north. He thinks to himself "a lot seems to be going on over there for it to be this early in the morning".

Baka and Nanki drive on up to the WISC Complex area. They pull up to the Main Front Gate and stop. The Security Office asks Baka where too. Main Storage Warehouse Sir and hands him his truck manifest. The Security Officer checks it out against his Checkoff list. Mr. Baka what you have onboard your truck is not on my list: (this was expected). Mr. Baka will you get out of your truck and open your main cab shell tail gate for me. Yes Sir. Baka does this and begins to worry somewhat. He tells the Security Officer Sir if there is a problem please call the Main Warehouse Manager at this CPH number WH 804. He can clear it up for us.

The Security Officer calls the CPH warehouse number WH 804. Hello Main Storage Warehouse Manager how may I help you? Sir I have a truck at the Main Front Gate destine for your location but I do not have the truck or its onboard cargo listed on my checkoff list as arriving today. Officer is the onboard cargo a wooden crate and is the crate marked with a special decal picture showing an American Bald Eagle Head mounted on Driftwood. Yes Sir it sure does! Great! Officer please pass that truck on through we have been waiting two days now for that crate to be delivered. Yes Sir right away, will do!

Officer while I am at I need to tip you off that this incoming crate is an exchange item. Langley Field Research Center delivered a similar incorrect crate to us by mistake. This same truck will be taking the incorrect crate back out and returning it to Langley Field and of course that crate will not appear on your checkoff list. Yes sir I understand. All straight folks go on in, drive straight down this road. The Main Storage Warehouse is the large building on the left you can't miss it. Great! Thank you Sir!

Baka and Nanki drive on down the roadway to the Main Storage Warehouse location. To Baka's surprise they are met out front by the Warehouse manager who has the doors open and waves them quickly inside. He waves them over by some Black curtains marked Bay 10, labeled "Driftwood Eagle".

Baka and Nanki step out as the Manager nods and tells them to move quickly as all three of them struggle to unload the heavy crate off the truck and sit it in place next to the other two crates. Damn Nanki Dewey did a great job all three crates match except Dewey's crate has the "Driftwood Eagle" decals installed upside down. All three then load up one of the other crates that contain the Prototype Exoset Missile Components. They check the two remaining Crates sitting there to make sure they appear undisturbed and in place. The manager nods good job guys, good bye and motions for them to quickly get the Hell out of there.

Baka slowly drives out of the Warehouse as the doors shut behind him. He drives up to the Main Front Gate and stops as required! The same Security Officer is still on duty! The Officer walks around to the rear of the truck and glances in; he sees the similar crate and recognizes the "Driftwood Eagle" decals. He walks back up front and waves Baka on through the gate. Baka drives on down the road and looks over at Nanki: SOB Nanki there for a while I thought our fuckin luck had run out! Me too! Shit, I started shaking like a junk yard dog shitting broken glass. Well Nanki we have the worse part of this crate exchange behind us let's head for the Cedar View Farm and the "Elsa Cree" and get this job over with.

Baka and Nanki finally arrive at the Cedar View Farm. They drive on down the long winding lane straight to the water front and main pier where the "Elsa Cree" is docked. They stop get out and start unloading the crate containing the Prototype Exoset missile Components. They struggle as it is a lot heavier than expected. They finally get it loaded on the main deck and lower it down to the hold level. They secure it tightly in place and cover it with the water proof tarp. Baka looks at Nanki and say's "man what a job but we got it done let's get the fuck out of here and go drink a few cold beers. Baka you got my vote!

Baka calls Doc up at the ARMA School House. Doc this is Baka! Baka how did it go? Piece a cake Doc your "Driftwood Eagle" exchange job is complete. No problems thanks to your inside POC and his CPH Warehouse number you gave me. Wonderful Baka great job Rahism Badhdadi will be overjoyed that's for sure. "Praise be to Allah"! Baka just think; Prototype Exoset Missile (Driftwood Eagle) Exchange Complete, High Yield Round Stick Dynamite Bomb set in place complete; what a great day for our Cell the "Delly Rode" Thank you again Baka your and Nanki did well go sip a few cold beers on me!!!!!!

Chapter 21

SPC INVESTIGATIONS CONTINUE

December 04, 2007 Tuesday morning. Susan finally wakes up. Hon what time is it? It's 0900Hr! What, you let me sleep that late! Well you were sleeping so peacefully and we had such a long day yesterday I knew you were worn out and could use the extra rest.

What have you been doing? Just sitting here looking out at the traffic, thinking and trying to gather up all my hunches, clues and pieces and put all them together. Susan I wonder if we really have a major "Delly Rode" al-Qaida Cell over here on the "Eastern Shore" or just a few al-Qaida trouble making thugs and POS? Susan nothing we have seen convinces me that a major cell planning serious missions over here exists. Yet for some reason my hunches tell me otherwise and I feel deep down inside something is being planned, something is going on. Well John based on experience your hunches always seem to work out let's go for it.

What plans do you have in place for us today? Well first thing I think we should do is go back across the road and check out the ARMA School House once more. Then I feel like we should just walk around and check out Dewey's Junk Yard Operation. Why the junk yard? What do you think may be important over there? What could be over at an old junk yard other than junk? Who knows!

Well Hon, let me run this by you. This morning very early I was looking across the road and I saw what I believe to be Allen Rasoul pull out of Dewey's side driveway and drive over to his school house and park. Following right behind him was a big Ford F-250 truck. It pulled out and headed north up Rt 13 carrying a heavy load as she was down a bit on her overload springs. It puzzles me, what would an educated man like Allen Rasoul be doing up and in an old junk yard at 0530Hr on a cold December morning? Well my dear little "Dick Tracy" tell you what, first let's go and eat a big breakfast; come back here and put ourselves into our SPC DIS go investigate and see what we can find out. Good Idea let's go!

Nerdy's room no. 1 house phone rings! Hello! Nerdy you old SOB it's me Don. Don where are you? Right here in Room Number 4 lower level front. Mela, Cela and me just checked in. Hell I am in Room Number 1 front. I know you AH I just dialed your room number. Nerdy just laughs, hell Don I am so use to using my CPH I forgot. Look, me and the girls are going to run over to the Delmarva Inn Restaurant for breakfast after everyone takes a big pee. We will meet you over there. Great, I will see you guys in a few minutes.

Nerdy walks into the restaurant. They all see him coming and wave him over. Don and Mela jump up and each give him a big hug. Damn Nerdy it is so good to see you, you look great! Nerdy this is my twin sister Cela! Wow, you two girls are truly identical twins that's for sure. Nerdy cannot believe how beautiful Cela is. He thinks to himself "she is stunning".

A cute waitress strolls up, good morning Nerdy did you sleep well? They all laugh as Nerdy turns red as a beet. Nerdy reply's with a weak "yes Tessie"! Tessie these folks are friends of mine from up in the Arlington, Virginia area. Good morning guys nice to meet you all; what will it be? Nerdy tells them all to order up, he is buying. He tells Tessie to put it all on his room bill. Nerdy say's "Gang May I suggest we start with the Delmarva Inn Bloody Mary" it's' to die for Tessie agrees; big secret they put a big table spoon full of crushed bacon in each glass".

Over on the far side of the restaurant Anna and Jamil have just finished eating and are getting up to leave. Anna looks over and spots Nerdy and his group of friends and decides to walk over to say hello and to meet them.

Lucky for Don he sees them coming over and recognizes Jamil right off. He is totally shocked to see him as he puts his hat back on along with his dark sunglasses and looks down in order to disguise himself as much as possible. He reaches in his shirt pocket and takes out his small ink pen and removes the cap. The ink pen is of course the small disguised twenty two caliber pistol Mela gave him when they were assigned to the Wood Duck Ridge (WDR) Mission.

Anna nods to Nerdy and introduces herself to the others. She introduces Jim Jamil as an old High School class mate. She tells them "that Jamil is enrolled as a full time student at the ARMA School across the road". They all chat for a few minutes then Anna and Jim Jamil say good bye and leave. Mela looks at Don (as he recaps his ink pen with a sigh of relief and puts it back in his pocket); and says "sweetheart you look like you just saw a ghost"!!!!! Mela I did believe me! Folks after we finish eating breakfast I would like for all of us to meet in our room No. 4, I have something very important I need to you tell you all!

Back at Mela, Cela and Don's room No. 4; Nerdy ask Don "for God's sake what's wrong, what got into back there in the restaurant". Don shakes a little as he tells them; fellows that Jim Jamil is a cruel, murdering, terrorist PAS. I can assure you he is not a full time student; that is BS and just a fuckin front. Mela and Cela, that ruthless SOB was second in command at "The Rock Cell" WDR area working under Abraham Rasoul. Both of these men were very cruel and treated your dad, me and your two brothers terrible.

Don do you think he may have recognized you? No Nerdy I don't think so, he did not show any signs of being surprised in the restaurant plus every time he has ever seen me I have had a long beard, dirty clothes, and dirty long hair and was wearing dark sunglasses! Don what do you plan on doing? Well some of the first things I need to find out is; why is he here, how did he get here, and how in earth did he survive that terrible WDR Earthquake?

Well guy's before we go anywhere I need to notify the U.S. Army Intelligence Office and Research Headquarters (Intell) right away; check in and get further instructions and advice from them. Don does this texting his message using his CPH and Secret Intell Code Numbers at Langley, Virginia. Langley Intell accepts his text message. Don's texts message of course tells Intell about meeting Jamil here today and gives them his location. Intell texts Don right back! Their reply reads: "our latest report has Jamil listed as killed in the WDR Earthquake, he is no longer any value to us, confirm his identification and watch his movements and if need be just kill the bastard." Well gang there you have it, you guys just keep a low profile, stay on guard and let me handle Mr. Jim Jamil my own way on my own terms. Like Mom always said "it comes home"!

Nerdy we did not come all the way over here to conduct Army Intell business; where would you folks like to go and what would you like to see and do? We have a beautiful day in front of us. Hell let's just ride around and take in and see this beautiful Eastern Shore Region of Virginia. Sounds great let's get going!!! Don before we leave let me ask you a personal question! Go ahead Nerdy! When did you realize Mela was the girl for you? Hell Nerdy that's an easy one; on our first date when I went to pick her up she opened the front door and was standing there totally naked holding a case of cold beer. Done Deal, My Kind of Gal! Nerdy gets embarrassed and calls Don an AH. He tells Mela you have got to watch this PAS! I know! As they all laugh! Let's go!

Susan and John return back to their room no.3 after breakfast! They put themselves into their SPC DIS leave and slowly walk across the road to the ARMA School Building. They walk right in; Maryrose is in her office working as usual and talking to the ARMA Assistant Director Abey Shawel. Doc is gone and so is his new Ford F-150 truck. They walk into Doc's office snooping around through his desk, cabinets everywhere they can find just looking and trying to locate any evidence what so ever relating to a Terrorist Cell. There clipped on Doc's desk calendar is a note. It reads; Secret Meeting at the Barn SRR on December 07, 2007 Friday 1500Hr. Hell Susan I was hoping we would be back home by then but it looks like we may be attending a meeting at the Barn. What Barn and where is this Barn located? We need to find out! Susan I have seen enough of this place for now, how about you? I am good to go, let's get out of here.

Susan and John leave and walk towards Dewey's Junk Yard. John stops, wait just a minute dear. What now? John takes out his CP puts it to his head and thinks ARMA School New Church, Virginia. Bingo, it rings. Maryrose picks up! Hello ARMA Maryrose here how may I help you? John in a disguised voice say's "Maryrose this is (Betsy Myers) can you help me I am totally lost? I am down here at the Exmore Post office. Doctor Rasoul told me to meet him at the Barn. How do I get to the Barn from here"? Betsy its nearby just take Rt 183 towards Silver Beach and the Chesapeake Bay. Doc Rasoul's Cedar View Farm is about two miles down that road on the right. "Thank you Maryrose, good bye"! Damn Susan this old SPC CP is hard to beat. I know, I told Helen she could have my old CPH I have another new one I like using a lot better.

Susan and John continue to walk on down Dewey's long side driveway. Damn Susan this is one big ass junk yard. I know they say it's the largest Junk Yard on the East coast. Hell I can believe that! They finally arrive at a large shop with a sign over the garage door that reads "Dewey's Chop Shop". Susan that damn JC always assigns me to missions that require a lot of walking. Hell hon I will be sixty one years old in April and all of this walking is a lot of BS. Stop bitchin all of this walking is good for us, just ask "Doctor Sterling"! "Fuck Sterile" his fat ass does not walk anywhere HA! HA!

Susan and John open the door and walk on in to the Dewey Chop Shop as if they own it. Not a soul in sight. Damn Susan look at the size of this place. Hell it must be twenty plus cars and trucks in here waiting to be stripped down for used parts, engines, transmissions and plain junk. They walk to the back and go through a door that leads to a separate wood working area. Damn Susan this area is set up for wood working only, look at all the tools; radial arm saws, band saws, belt sanders, drill presses, you name it Dewey has it all. Don't get any ideas John you have all the tools at home you need already! John walks over to the far end of the wood working area and stops at a long table like bench. He glances at all of the left over scrap material lying around. All of a sudden his thoughts and hunches begin to materialize. He shouts to Susan" SOB Hon come over here and look at this, we just "HIT PAY DIRT", Like Old Richard said "Miss Rudolf Gonna Get Her Fuckin Turkey"!!!!! You can bet your sweet ass on that!

Chapter 22

SPC HITS PAY DIRT

December 04, 2007 Tuesday afternoon. Still in Dewey's Chop Shop wood working area Susan all excited runs over to see what John has found out that causes him to shout "HIT PAY DIRT"!!! John what have you found? Look here, sitting on this work bench six empty "High Yield Dynamite Round Stick Boxes"! Check out "The From labeling" on the boxes; ACME ORDRANCE COMPANY, Hamlin, New York. Also check out "The To labeling"; Justin Conyers's Road Construction Company. Fishersville, Virginia. Susan all of this confirms that a Terrorist Cell does exist over here on the Eastern Shore of Virginia, JC and Lt Ree were correct. How large is this cell, who knows we will just have to wait, look, see and find out.

Susan this High Yield Round Stick Dynamite is the remains from the Conyers Construction Site robbery that took place back in September. Adam Rasoul received five cases and we now know his brother Allen Rasoul received the other five cases. Adam Rasoul had one case left in the casket inside his 1941 Packard Hearse when we let him and Javid escape from Topper's Air Field on Halloween night. I could have kicked my own ass later as I should have taken that one case when I had the chance. Like the man said "You Can't Fix Stupid"!

Look here at these CPU 3-DI CD Print Outs of the Prototype Exoset Special Shipping Crate. John picks up a big envelope, Susan it looks like you are going to get your wish after all as he looks at the four remaining prints of the "Driftwood Eagle" decals and hands her the envelope. These are left over from this package of six decals.

Susan my dear my hunches are paying off and the pieces of this puzzle are beginning to fit together just look at these left over wood scraps. These Terrorist POS have constructed a duplicate wooden missile crate using this CPU 3-DI CD information. They have packed it full of this stolen High Yield Dynamite and wired it up using one of these wired donator caps. When completed they place the two missing "Driftwood Eagle" decals on the outside of the crate to match.

John I know what you are thinking and it is all very clear! These no good AH have developed a Bomb that resembles a wooden Prototype Exoset Missile crate. Yes and not only that my dear containing one hundred and forty four sticks of High Yield Dynamite Round Sticks; that enough explosive force to blow the Wallops Island Complex off this "Beautiful God Given Earth" of ours. They have already or will I am sure transport this bomb up to the WISC Complex and try to exchange it for one of the two existing crates we saw in place yesterday that contain the real Prototype Exoset Missile Components ASAP. A perfect Hijack Job! Damn Susan it just occurred to me I just bet that big overloaded Ford F-250 I saw pulling out from here this morning early and turning north was transporting this crated Bomb. Could be! Damn hon if they set off a Bomb of that size they will kill and injure hundreds of innocent people plus the explosive force from that much High Yield Dynamite will create millions of dollars in collateral damage throughout this entire area.

Susan I have seen all I need to see over here, gather up your "Driftwood Eagle" decals and whatever, let's get the hell out of here. We need to go back up to the WISC Complex PDQ. Hon we have our work cut out for us! I do not know if the duplicate crate exchange has taken place or not? We will soon find out! If my hunch is correct my guess is it has, based on that big Ford F-250 truck that left Dewey's junk yard this morning. When these Terrorist thugs plan their so called "Big Bang" to take place as they like to call it is another problem we need to solve ASAP. If a crate exchange has already taken place the "Big Bang" will take place soon you can bet on that. These terrorist POS know that they cannot wait too long as the WISC Complex ordnance engineers will investigate and discover the duplicated exchanged crate when they start setting up the Prototype Exoset Missile Tests Programs.

Susan and John quickly leave Dewey's Junk Yard and walk back over to their Delmarva Inn Room they go in and convert themselves back into a human state. They get in their old Ford F-150 truck and drive quickly on up to the WISC Complex. John you better slow down or you are going to get stopped by the VASP and get a ticket, settle down: what will be will be. I know, I know! I am just excited about this breakthrough. What a lucky break.

They arrive at the WISC visitor's area pull in and park as before. John looks around no one in sight, coast is clear as they again put themselves into their SPC DIS. SOB more walking but having been here before they know exactly where to go. They finally arrive at the Main Storage Warehouse and walk right in. Damn this place is loaded with people working at their jobs. With all the new drones, planes and rockets on line to be tested there is a large amount of work scheduled to take place. The average man on the street has no idea what really goes on at a test facility of this size.

Susan and John slowly walk over to the Black Curtains marked Bay 10 labeled "Driftwood Eagle". Behind the curtains there they sit two identical crates just like yesterday. Now they must examine these crates to determine if an exchange has actually taken place. Were the al-Qaida terrorist thugs experienced enough and smart enough to pull off their planned crate exchange job and Hijack an Exoset Prototype Missile right under the watchful eyes of the WISC Complex Security Force? We will soon find out, I certainly hope not!

Damn Susan these two crates are Identical a perfect match. If an exchange has taken place one contains about One hundred and Twenty pounds of High Yield Dynamite the other Five Sealed Hypergolic Containers of Prototype Exoset Missile Components. All I can say if an exchange has taken place Dewey did a remarkable job of crate duplication. He sure did! Do you see any physical differences between the crates? No not really! Hell may be the Hijacking scheme was discovered and did not take place after all, who knows?

Susan and John continue to walk around Bay 10 and investigate the entire area as well as the two crates. Susan I am convinced these are the same two crates we found yesterday I do not believe an exchange has taken place yet. John I believe you are right. Susan I may have to take a chance and use my CP to view the interior of these crates to solve our problem.

John please do not do that if your SPC CP Laser should accidently strike an existing detonator cap you could blow this whole place to hell and back. John it's not worth the risk let's just leave keep our eyes and ears open and return later. We now know that a terrorist cell does exist and we know what they have planned. Let's just go and concentrate our Investigation efforts on Dewey's Junk Yard and Allen Rasoul's ARMA School House, sit tight and just see what happens. I agree my dear we have time let's go and come back later tonight and take another survey.

As they begin to walk away Susan looks at John's disappointed face then takes one last look at the crates. She screams and laughs out loud. Surrounding WISC employees close by look at each other and wonder where in the hell is all that screaming and laughter coming from; they just shrug it off and go back to work. For God's sake Susan what the hell was that all about? Susan gets control of herself and settles down. John we are two dumb asses don't you see the differences in the two crates? Hell no smart ass, do you? Yes I do my dear little "Dick Tracy". The duplicate wooden crate constructed by Dewey's has the "Driftwood Eagle" decals pasted on it upside down!!!! SOB how do you like that, hon I could not see the forest for the trees. Mrs. SPC Agent VA10C you did well! Do not get upset my dear there have been other times in the past that you have not been the sharpest knife in the draw, HA! HA! Funny, Funny Miss Wonderful!!!!!

They both settle down and are relieved that they have found the exchanged crate and finally get themselves back to the serious business at hand. Hon, help me survey this crate for any signs of metal pins protruding from the inside out; they will need those in order to charge the detonator cap and set off the dynamite bomb inside.

John what is the purpose of those pins and how do they work? Well the stupid al-Qaida terrorist bastard that plans on blowing himself up and committing suicide (Martyrdom) for the cause has a small transmitter. This transmitter is similar to an automatic garage door opener; it has two connecting wires that he attaches to these exposed pins using common old alligator clips. All he needs to do then is press the transmitter button in the name of Allah and at the same time bend over and kiss his stupid dumb ass good bye, done deal. Susan how do you fuck seventy two virgins when your dick is plastered all over the ceiling of this warehouse? Beats me!

John have you found anything yet? No, just keep looking they are here somewhere. Here they are; Dewey attached one of the crate oak wood, lifting handles using brass stud bolts that protrude and the other one using standard flathead wood screws, smart guy old trick. These brass stud bolts are your detonator pins standard procedure. John takes out his SPC CP and aims the laser at each stud bolt one at a time this heats up the brass metal bolt hot enough so that the attached soldered interior pulsating wires detach break loose and fall safely away. With this done and a conduction check he now knows conduction cannot take place to set off the High Yield Dynamite Round Sticks packed inside. Susan my dear we did it; the "Delly Rode Cell" al-Qaida Terrorist dynamite bomb has been successfully defused. Let's get the fuck out of here I need a cold beer. John my dear you just got my vote let's go!

Back in their old Ford F-150 truck they look around, coast is clear as they convert themselves back to a human state. Damn this SPC DIS is one powerful weapon thank the Good Lord it belongs to us and not those towel heads, TYDL

Susan this "Delly Rode" Cell crowd is a sharp group of folks. Do you realize they developed a bomb, transported it and exchanged it for a secret Prototype Exoset Missile right under the noses of some of the best Security Forces the WISC Complex has in place. Kind of scares the hell out of you! Yes it does, but what do we do next the more we look the worse it seems to get? Susan you just keep getting it and keep going it never ends but my dear never give up!

Susan three things we need to find out ASAP is; One, where is the "Delly Rode Cell's" main base of operations over here on the "Eastern Shore; Two, where have they taken that crate loaded with those Prototype Exoset missile Components they just Hijacked and Three, what time do they plan on setting off that crated dynamite bomb they exchanged at the WISC Complex we just defused. Fine I agree John, but one thing I do not understand is why you aren't going to notify the WISC Complex Security Office and tell them about the crated bomb we located in Bay10? Susan if I / we do that the al-Qaida agent or agents working inside the WISC Complex will get suspicious know they have been discovered and haul ass and live to kill another day. I do not want that, I want to confront those bastards and take their fuckin asses out; dead, is dead.

Well my dear what do we do now? We go back to our room drink a few cold beers and rest. Later we go over to the Delmarva Inn restaurant for supper and pig out on their big seafood buffet. On the way to our room we need to stop by the front desk and get our room reservations extended for at least through the eighth of December. Remember Friday the seventh we will be attending Allen Rasouls's secret 1500Hr meeting at the Barn SRR.

Susan my hunches tell me that meeting may be the answer to most of our questions, "I feel it will be the icing on the cake". John I feel the same way, TYDL. I hope so!

John and Susan after a long tiring very eventful day finally get back to their Room No. 3. John unlocks the door and steps in; as he does he sees an envelope lying on the floor that someone slipped in through the door mail slot. The envelope has Room No. 4 marked on it, shit wrong room some dumb AH fucked up. Curious he opens and reads the note in side as the envelope was not sealed. The note reads; Don, Jim Jamil has been ordered by the "Delly Rode Cell" to eliminate "Nerdy" on or before Friday December the 7th. John shows the note to Susan. Now what? Don't worry I will look into this ASAP.

As John and Susan leave to go to the Restaurant he adds a note of his own to the note in the envelope. He slips the envelope in the door slot of Room No.4 as they pass by. Susan nods her approval and states "does it ever end"!! No my dear it never will!!!!!

Chapter 23

SAVE "NERDY"

December 04, 2007 Tuesday afternoon late. Don Gear pulls in to his Room No.4 parking place in front of the Delmarva Inn. Man, I sure do like getting our room on the ground level up front! You drive right on up to your front door, can't beat that plus no stairs to climb.

Well everyone it's 1800Hr anyone ready for a night cap? Nerdy how about you? I am with the crowd. I tell you what let's just go in to the bar unwind a little, sip a couple of beers and call it a night it has been a long tiring day for everyone. They all agree great idea!

Nerdy heads quickly for his Room No. 1. Mela, Cela and Don also haul ass for their Room No.4. Nerdy says "sorry folks for leaving so fast but I really need to urinate"! Don says "don't you mean piss"! They all laugh at Nerdy as you cannot help but like the guy he is such a sweet innocent person. I will meet you guy's in the Bar! OK Nerdy!

Don unlocks the door to their Room No.4 as he steps in he sees the envelope and picks it up. Mela asks what is that all about? I don't know. As they read the note inside Mela and Cela begin to get upset and cry. Will this terror ever end? Don we need to get Nerdy somewhere safe and away from this place ASAP. I know you ladies just stay calm for now and keep your eyes and ears open. Don reads John's added note it reads; this was delivered to our Room No.3 by mistake. I took the liberty to read it. Please call me I may be able to help and give you some advice.

Don, Mela and Cela walk over to the bar. But after reading the note the luster of the evening has been lost and the excitement has disappeared. Don tells the girls "act like you have not read this note and please do not say a word to Nerdy about the note". I will take care of things later.

Nerdy walks in happy as a fat little pig in mud! Hey Nerdy, long time no see I miss you. Damn Cela you are a piece of work. You just keep it up and I am going to take you home to mama. Be careful what you say Nerdy I just might say yes and go with you. They all laugh! After a few beers they all begin to loosen up a bit. Nerdy how long are you planning to be in town? Anna Belle and I will be flying out Friday morning early. Straight from WISC back to Langley Field, in Hampton Virginia then on to the AEA in Las Vegas. Well we still have a few more days together can you handle that? Yes as long as it includes Cela. Cela just laughs as she is getting very attached to Nerdy and thinks he is cute and adorable.

Nerdy I have a surprise for you. You do, what is that Don? Well we are also leaving Friday morning to go back to Arlington, Virginia. But the big surprise is: Mela, Cela and I are taking leave on December the 21st, 2007 through January 03, 2008. We have already made reservation to fly to Las Vegas to spend Christmas and New Years with my parents. SOB you are kidding me! No way! Well as you know my folks live there full time. Damn Don I completely forgot about that. Yes, I am going to take my beautiful Mela home and show her off to my folks. Don that is wonderful. What a wonderful Christmas and New Years that will be for you both. Nerdy what are your holiday plans? While in Vegas we all will want to see and spend some time with you if you are available? Well I was going to go home to upper state New York and spend a long Christmas and New Year's Holiday with my family but that has just changed as of now. I will now just spend Christmas Eve and Christmas Day at home. I will fly back to Vegas and meet you guys at Bud's Place late on the 26 of December how about them apples! They all laugh, your mom's going to think you are an AH. No she will understand "She La me" HA! HA! Well we will see you in Vegas at Bud's Place on the twenty sixth of December. Great I will be there with bells on that's for sure!

Well folks it has been a long wonderful day but I have had enough and need to turn in. I will meet you guys at the restaurant at 0900Hr tomorrow morning for a big buffet breakfast. Great Nerdy we will see you then. Wait Nerdy as Cela jumps up and runs over gives him a big hug and a good night kiss; sleep tight don't let the bed bugs bite! Highly embarrassed Nerdy says good night and leaves. Don. Mela, Cela soon follow as they too are worn out from their long sightseeing day on the "Eastern Shore". Don goes to pay the check. The Clerk tells him it's already been paid. Who paid it as if he did not know? Some nice looking nerdy type guy! They all laugh and leave.

When they return back to their Room No. 4 Don lets the girls in and tells Mela "you and Cela go do your triple "S" I have some very important business I need to attend too. Mela understands and just tells "Don to be careful and that she loves him". He kisses her good night winks and says "I love you too" and leaves!

Don goes next door and knocks on the door of Room No.3. John watching TV and sipping on a cold beer looks over at Susan; who the hell can that be at this time of night? John asks who is it! Don reply's you do not know me but my name is Don Gear and I got your note. John lets Don in and shakes his hand. Don introduces himself to Susan and John. Susan gets them all a cold beer. Don briefly tells John a few things about himself and why he is in town.

Don let's cut to the chase and get right down to business. Fine with me John fire away! Don who sent you that note? I have no idea! Who is Jim Jamil? John he is one of the cruelest PAS on this PE. He is an al-Qaida murdering terrorist SOB! Don where do you know him from and how do you know all of this? Don proceeds to tell Susan and John briefly all about his job, his WDR experience in Afghanistan and "The Rock Cell"; and of course the actions of Jamil while there. John and Susan are not strangers to The WDR Mission but being SPC Agents and sworn to secrecy of course cannot speak to Don about any of John's involvement and how the WDR Earthquake developed. Don do you know the location of Jim Jamil at this time and where he might be staying? John he resides right here in the ARMA Student Dorm Section of the Delmarva Inn in Room No. 301. John would you believe the al-Qaida Terrorist Group have assigned this man to assassinate my good and dear friend Cedric Fauntleroy a.k.a. "Nerdy"? Do you guys by chance know Cedric? No not really we have seen him here and know of him, that is all. Don why would the local al-Qaida cell want to eliminate him? John they have continually tried to recruit him to their service and cause because of his excellent knowledge related to Aerospace Technology. He is an Albert Einstein / Von Braun combined inside but a little pussy cat on the outside. John Nerdy is a True Blue American Patriot and would give his life for his beloved U.S.A. I know this for a fact as he worked with me in the U.S. Army Intell Service. John it's simple if they cannot recruit him the next step is to remove him and take away his knowledge and service from us.

John like I just told you I have served with Nerdy and worked with him at DAE at AEA in Las Vegas, Nevada. I would die for him. I notified my superiors in Langley, Virginia earlier they gave me clear orders to watch Jim Jamil and eliminate him if need be. He is just another al-Qaida towel head PAS. John I am prepared to do this, I have done this before with no problems or regrets.

Don I have some friends in key, low and high places if you will. Hold off doing anything and stay put for a few days and let me make a couple of CPH. Go now, I will be in touch; keep a low profile Jamil may have recognized you if he makes any threating moves take him out but for now let me handle this. Don thanks John and Susan for their concerns and time. He shakes John's hand, gives Susan a hug and leaves. He is now content as he knows good people like Susan and John has his back.

After Don leaves John calls Lt Ree at SPCEBS and discusses the entire case involving Jamil. John let me call you back I need to check out a few things and run this by JC. Lt Ree it's now 2000Hr can you get back to me before 2400Hr? John I will do my best good bye! John what did Lt Ree say? He will check out some things and call me right back: I think I will get another cold beer just sit back and wait on his call. Well my dear I am going to soak in a big hot bath let me know what you plan on doing next and if you need me for anything! Thank you my dear.

John no sooner gets his beer and sits down as his CP vibrates; damn it's Lt Ree calling back already. Lt Ree what have you got for me? John I called JC he was very aware of Jim Jamil from reading all of our WDR Earthquake reports. Like you he thought the WDR Earthquake Mission eliminated the worthless PAS. JC told me to tell you to take the SOB out ASAP he is of no value to us or anyone else anymore. Thank you Lt Ree old buddy you just made my fuckin day.

John takes his time and finishes his beer then proceeds to put himself into his SPC DIS. He pokes his head in the bathroom and tells Susan he will be back in a few minutes. John for God's sake where in the hell are you going its 2330Hr. My dear I am going for a short walk over to Room No. 301. I need to take care of a Terrorist PAS we missed somehow on the

WDR Mission. His name is Sgt Jim Jamil. Great, but can't it wait until tomorrow? No way; the lives of two first class young men may be at stake. We'll be careful dear, I love you! I love you too!

John leaves his room and walks down to the corner stairwell He climbs the steps to the third floor level and walks around the outside balcony to the ARMA leased dormitory section. He walks on over to the last room on the left, Room No. 301. He stops and quietly listens, not a sound and no one in sight. Being in his SPC DIS he just walks in as if he owns the room and sits down, looks around, waits and listens.

John looks at and assumes the nude man sitting on the bed is Jim Jamil. The bathroom door opens and to his surprise Anna Belle walks out totally in the nude still drying herself off using her bath towel. John thinks to himself "damn Anna is beautiful I cannot believe that ugly bastard is getting all that milk and honey". She lies down on the bed and looks at the man as he is up and getting dressed. Jim Jamil what the hell is wrong with you? You SOB I just got all cleaned up and I am ready for a little sexual activity my old puss is bubbling like a hard crab and here you are getting dressed ready to go out. Hell thirty minutes ago you said "you were hot to trot for some pie at the "Y". Hell I get all ready so you could have me and now you are leaving. You AH "where in the hell are you going at this time of night its 2345Hr for God's sake"?

Anna calm down I will be right back just keep the milk, honey and pie warm! Hell at least tell me where are you going? To Room No.1 ground floor to take care of some al-Qaida assigned business. Hell that's Nerdy's room! I know so what he is just a low life infidel PAS I will take care of him and be right back. Anna I need to put this al-Qaida assignment behind me and get it off my mind it's beginning to bug me. Like I said "calm down and keep the pie warm I will be right back".

John now knowing he has the right man leaves the room and waits outside. He looks through the front window of the room and watches as Jim Jamil loads his 9mm automatic pistol and installs a firelight silencer. Jamil steps outside the room and stands, he takes his time and just looks around, it's so quiet you can hear a pin drop. John thinks to himself "you got here just in time you will save Nerdy's smart, valuable little ass from this assassinating murdering bastard", TYDL!

Anna totally pissed off quickly jumps up from the bed picks up the house phone and calls Nerdy's Room No.1. Nerdy answers and in an unusual nasty tone says "who is the AH calling me at this hour, it's midnight and I was in bed fast asleep what the hell do you want? Anna muffles a little and disguises her voice! Mr. Fauntleroy this is the Delmarva Inn Security Office: sir we are sorry to disturb you at this late hour but we have some uninvited visitors on the grounds that we are trying to locate! "Please do not open your Room Door to anyone for any reason until we call you back"! I will comply. Thank you for calling sorry about my rude language!

As Anna completes her call she hangs up the phone and begins to cry. Sad to say she is a very confused young girl. She is a sworn well trained al-Qaida agent but she is having mixed emotions and second thoughts about remaining and staying a member. She understands Nerdy is considered an infidel and she has pledged herself to Allah and her support to the al-Qaida cause. She adores Nerdy and in his case wants his life spared if possible. She knows making that phone call was wrong and if she is found out it could cost her, her life but what else could she do??? She felt she needed to protect and save Nerdy. Will this terror ever stop?

Jim Jamil walks over to the balcony railing and looks out, no one in sight not a sound. John steps up behind Jamil and gently touches his neck. Jamil dies instantly from a SPC induced silent heart attack drops and slopes over the balcony railing. His dead body trembles as it tumbles over the railing and strikes the concrete driveway three stories below face first. John thinks to himself "the way Jamil's body went over the railing, the vertical fall and his ugly fuckin face hitting that hard concrete the way it did has to be scored a PERFECT 10". Jim Jamil you damn dumb ass you should have stayed in bed with that beautiful Anna had you milk and honey and ate that juicy pie at the "Y" like a big boy. Dear GOD forgive me I know killing is wrong but I sure do enjoy eliminating these al-Qaida towel head low life terrorist POS!

John returns to his room, he quietly unlocks the door and goes in thinking Susan is in bed asleep. Hon, is that you? No it a strange man sneaking in to ravage your beautiful fifty five year old body before Big John returns. She laughs; I wish, how did it go? Piece a cake a Perfect fuckin 10 from all the judges you should have been there. Hon I did get a big surprise, guess who was in bed shacking up with Jamil; Anna Belle. Damn John was Jim Jamil that same sleazy looking guy we saw her with Monday in the lobby? Yes the one and the same. Do you think Anna Belle is an al-Qaida Agent? Susan I am not sure but I would bet the farm on it. "The Delly Rode" Cell received all of that Secret Prototype Exoset Missile information we found over at Dewey's Junk Yard Chop Shop from someone working inside the DAE company that's for damn sure. She was working inside the DAE on the Exoset Missile project full time as Nerdy's assistant and had access to all of it. It is a piece of the puzzle that seems to fit. When I discussed this Mission with Dennis, SPC Agent NV36C he told me then that Anna Belle was a suspect and that the SPCEBS and Zone 52 had her under investigation as a possible al-Qaida Agent.

December 05, 2007 Wednesday morning. Nerdy up early meets Mela, Cela and Don at the restaurant for breakfast. Good morning guys did you all sleep well and get well rested from our long day? Don replies, yes it's easy to sleep well cuddled up with my beautiful Mela how about you? Fine after I finally got back to sleep. The Delmarva Inn Security Office woke me up about midnight calling about some intruders on the grounds, did they call you guys? No, we did not get any phone calls from anyone! That' funny! Hell before I went back to sleep I heard sirens looked out front and saw an ambulance drive in and go around back followed by the Sheriff's car. I wonder what that was all about. Who knows?

The waitress walks up, good morning guys, Hi Nerdy did you sleep well? They all laugh as Nerdy turns beet red as usual. What can I get you folks this fine morning besides your usual Bloody Mary's? Tessie what do you suggest? How about our morning special; scrambled eggs with cream cheese and fresh cut basil with country ham on the side. Tessie that sounds great make it four orders! Folks coming right up pippin hot fresh off the old grill!

Tessie before you leave let me ask you; what happened around this place last night? Your Delmarva Security Office called my room about midnight and told me not to open my door to anyone and before I could go back to sleep an ambulance rescue squad and the Sheriff drive up. Damn Nerdy I do not know who may have called your room the Delmarva Inn does not even have a Security office. Hell things are so quiet around here in these parts we just rely on the Accomac County Sheriff's Office if we need law enforcement help of any kind. As far as the ambulance and Sheriff goes the night shift told me this morning that some poor soul either fell or jumped off of the third level balcony out back late last night and killed himself. Don asks, Tessie do you know who it might be? Yes one of our student guests named Jim Jamil staying in room 301. Don, Mela and Cela all look up to the ceiling and say in unison "Thank you Dear God," TYDL. Nerdy just shakes his head looks at them and mumbles "something funny is going on around here; I don't know about you guys you sure are acting very strange this morning". They all laugh and say Nerdy you do not have a need to know just sip on your Bloody Mary and thank God you are here with us!!! And we are all here together safe and sound.

John and Susan walk in. Don sees them and waves them over to meet his friends. Good morning folks. John and Susan I would like you to meet my friends as Don introduces everyone. John did you and Susan hear the news about the tragic accident they had here late last night? Yes we sure did what a shame! John looks at Don Winks and gives him thumbs up. Don when you have friends in key, low and high places things like that can and will happen. Nerdy still lost just shakes his head some more. Well nice to meet you all. Mela looks at Don and tells him hon you have tears running down you cheeks. Mela it's nothing something just got in my eyes I am OK! We'll let us go you kids have a nice day and stay safe nice to meet you all. Thank you Mr. and Mrs. James you have a nice day too!

Chapter 24

SPECIAL DELLY RODE CELL MEETING

December 07, 2007 early Friday morning. Nerdy, Don, Mela and Cela are all up early a quick breakfast behind them, packed, checked out and standing outside in front of the Delmarva Inn ready to leave. All four say their good byes with a lot of big hugs and kisses. Cela gives Nerdy a big special kiss and thanks him for a wonderful three days. (Unbeknown to Nerdy being with him has helped her to continue to heal from the loss of Adrian Rasoul as she realizes her life must go on). Nerdy as usual after that big kiss on the lips lights up like a Christmas tree. Nerdy looks at her and states "Cela keep that up and you will have me at the "Y" kissing those other lips; you just wait. Miss Cela I am going to take you home to mama one of these days you just wait and see"! Nerdy where in the world did you learn to talk like that? Mela I learned it from that PAS standing right there you are going to marry, army talk. They all laugh and get ready to leave.

As Nerdy begins to drive away he shouts to them "I will see you guys at Buds Place in Vegas on the 26th of December". Nerdy pulls out and heads north up Rt 13, The Ole Delly Rode" towards the WISC Complex to meet up with Anna Belle and catch the first leg of their flight back to Langley Field then on home to Las Vegas.

As Nerdy slowly drives along he notices an envelope on the passenger side seat with his name on it. Curious about what it may say and be all about he safely pulls over off the road and stops to read it. He opens the envelope and takes out a note from Anna Belle. The note reads; Nerdy please give this note to Mr. Norman Savage and hopefully he will accept it as my official letter of resignation from the DAE Company. My short stay employed at the DAE was an experience I will never forget. This decision has been hard for me but I have decided to remain here and return to my beloved home in Williamsburg, Virginia. Nerdy working with you was wonderful, I adore you and you will always be on my mind and in my heart. I will keep in touch, Love Ya, Anna Belle.

Nerdy pulls back out on the road and continues to drive on to the WISC Complex. As he drives along he thinks to himself "this note from Anna seals it, bingo". My Intell training and experience had Anna pegged from the get go as an inside terrorist spy". Nerdy thinks to himself "My Dear Anna you cannot hide forever we will find out who you are working for and arrest you one day. It's obvious to me you are afraid and now on the run, so sad. Anna you are a wonderful girl and could have been somebody". Why! Why!

Don pulls out and also heads north back home towards Arlington, Virginia! It's been an exciting three days for everyone but all three will tell you the best part of the whole trip is to see Nerdy and now know he is safe and sound. Mela looks at Cela and says "my dear sister what did you think of our little Nerdy"? I like him very much! Mela like you said "he is a trip" and I will stay in touch with him that's for sure. Hell he might take me home to mama yet, who knows!!!!! They all laugh!

John what time do you have? It's 1200Hr! Don't you think we ought to get started for the meeting? Susan the Secret Special Delly Rode meeting does not start until 1500Hr we have plenty of time just calm down. I know but I am anxious to get there I just feel like it is going to be an exciting, mysterious and a strange experience for me. I am excited and ready to go!

Susan is finally relieved as they leave for the Cedar View farm and the secret meeting. John drives south slowly down the Ole Delly Rode and closely follows the instructions he received from Maryrose (via Betsy). They arrive at the Cedar View Farm with no problems except to find the driveway entrance is gated and locked. SOB now what? He drives on pass the Cedar View Farm entrance and as luck would have it spots a turnabout up a head. He pulls in parks and looks around, no one in sight. The coast is clear my dear as they put themselves into their SPC DIS. When they get out John takes an old rag and ties it around one door handle to suggest the truck is disabled and out of service.

SOB more fuckin walking! Damn Susan it's a fuckin mile back to the damn farm gate. John quit bitchin the walk will do us good, don't be so grumpy. May be so but how far is it to the Barn from the gate? At the gate they stop to rest for a moment just as Maryrose drives in and stops. As Maryrose fumbles around trying to punch in the gate code numbers John walks over and drops the tailgate on her small S-10 ARMA School truck. He and Susan sit down on the tailgate and ride on up to the Barn with Maryrose. Nice thinking "White Wing" as Susan pats him on the back!

Maryrose parks gets out of the truck and walks to the Barn and on over to the SRR. John and Susan follow her. It is now 1400Hr! Allen Rasoul is already there putting up chairs and setting things up! Maryrose gives him a hug and says are you all set and ready to go this is a biggie? Ready as I will ever be my dear.

It is now 1445Hr everyone that has been invited has arrived accept of course Jim Jamil. Allen Rasoul stands at the speakers stand and begins. Dear Friends and fellow Agents before I begin this most important meeting in the history of our beloved al-Qaida Delly Rode Cell; let's pause for a minute to praise our lost Agent Jim Jamil who was taken from us Tuesday night. Praise be to Allah! John whispers to Susan I wonder what happened to that PAS? John do you not have any compassion? No my dear not for these murdering bastards. God forgive me!

Allen calls the roll before he has Baka lock the security door: Maryrose, Anna Belle, Baka, Nanki, Manki, Rahism Badhdadi, my dear sister Dayzee and her husband Dewey Duzz and two special guests from the NNGA; Field Marshall's Adolf H. Goring and Adolf H. Junker. Everyone gasps as no one expected special guests from the Neo-Nazi German Army (NNGA) to be here. Even Susan and John are somewhat taken back. John whispers to Susan SOB, this is big; I wonder what this is all about and where did those two POS come from? Susan I did not see Anna Belle when she walked in but her being here now confirms the SPCEBS suspicion that she may be an al-Qaida Agent. Hell if I had this much proof Tuesday night I could have eliminated her at the same time along with Jim Jamil and killed two birds with one stone. No worry she will get hers in due time, that's for damn sure. Susan the puzzle is coming together with one piece still missing. What piece is that? Who is the suicide bomber or bombers (martyrdoms) working inside the WISC Complex assigned by this Delly Rode Cell to detonate that crated dynamite bomb we defused?

Allen Rasoul continues his presentation as he gets straight to the facts. Fellow Agents we had two prime missions planned. Both of these I am happy to tell you for the most part have been accomplished. One of these of course was to hijack a Prototype Exoset Missile. We did this with a lot of work by agents Baka, Nanki, Dewey Duzz and Anna Belle. That Hijacked Prototype Exoset Missile is safely secured and stowed onboard the Elsa Cree ready to be shipped to our Cuban Cell leader Lt Ramey Sanchez. Once there Lt Sanchez will make arrangements to have it transferred to the NNGA ASAP. Mission number two is something I have been thinking about and planning for years and that is to take down the WISC Complex and put it completely out of service. Again thanks to Nanki, Baka and Dewey Duzz. Together these three agents developed, constructed and exchanged a duplicated Exoset Missile Crated Bomb with a similar Exoset Missile Crate located in the WISC Main Storage Warehouse. We have available a brave martyrdom al-Qaida agent employed by the WISC Complex working inside who will glorify himself to Allah and set off this crated dynamite bomb on Wednesday afternoon January 02, 2008 at exactly 1430Hr.

Fellow al-Qaida Agents the reason I selected this "Big Bang" date and time is because at this time the WISC Complex Director Charles Nutmaker will present his yearly "State of The WISC Complex Address. The Main Storage Warehouse at that time will be set up as a temporary auditorium to seat at least one thousand plus WISC Complex employees and this of course is where the Director will present his address.

Just think when our inside POC detonates that crated bomb placed nearby most of these WISC working infidel POS will be blown to pieces. How great is that! "Praise Be to Allah"! Also with the amount of explosive dynamite materials Dewey was able to pack inside that crated bomb the collateral damage will level most of the WISC Complex. Again! "Praise Be to Allah"!

Any questions! Yes; Marshall Adolf Goring. No questions Allen except to congratulate you're wonderful "Delly Rode Cell" Agents for outstanding work. Thanks to your fortitude, planning and the leadership of Rahism Badhdadi my Neo-Nazi Party now have the Prototype Exoset Missile we need. I can tell you for a fact with the secret manufacturing facilities we have built underground in Santiago Cuba we can now duplicate and produce this weapon with no problems.

Allen Rasoul and Rahism Badhdadi I predicted a complete come back for your great al-Qaida Army and cause. Your forces along with our great Neo-Nazi German Army will no doubt rule the World one day; it's just a matter of time. One last thing Allen to express my appreciation and to support your great cause please except this early Christmas Gift from me and your Neo-Nazi Party friends. Everyone laughs as they all know Muslims do not observe a foolish myth like Christmas. Baka comes in carrying a beautiful Christmas wrapped MC and places it on the table in front of Allen, Allen weeps as he is so overcome with gratitude. What can I say except thank you so much Marshall Goring this was not expected; our "Delly Rode Cell" sure can use these beautiful Benny's.

Allen nods to Baka, Baka if you will, please take this MC up to my study in the big house and put it in my walk in closet for safe keeping I will take care of it later.

If no more questions I will close this meeting with this major announcement as discussed in full with our al-Qaida Caliphate Commander Rahism Badhdadi and NNGA Field Marshall Adolf H. Goring: The good ship the "Elsa Cree" will sail from my Cedar View Farm pier on Tuesday December the 25th, 2007. Departure time will be at 1600Hr. Destination Santiago Cuba! Listen up, hear me and follow these orders no questions asks, those persons making this trip are as follows: Rahism Badhdadi, Baka, Nanki, Manki, Anna Belle and Field Marshalls Adolf H. Goring and Adolf H. Junker.

Nanki and Manki as licensed Marine Pilots and Navigators you will operate the boat, Baka will control and handle all security, Anna Belle with support from Nanki will handle the galley and provide all the meals, Rahism Badhdadi will be in Full Command. Fellow al-Qaida let this be said and let it be done, Praise be to Allah! For now this meeting is adjourned let's all go to the Barn dormitory kitchen to sip a bit of good German beer, French Red wine and celebrate our good fortunes and give thanks to Allah.

Chapter 25

DRIFTWOOD EAGLE MISSION;
SHUT DOWN & TAKE OUT

December 07, 2007 Friday afternoon late. Susan and John stand up look at each other and state; we certainly got just about all the answers we came here looking for, a very informed meeting to say the least. As they prepare to leave the Secret Special Delly Rode al-Qaida Cell meeting John hesitates. Dear, before we leave let's just walk around snoop and check this place out a little bit we are in no hurry to leave. Susan you survey the Barn area especially the storage rooms and I will check out the big house. Meet me back over by Maryrose's S-10 truck in about thirty minutes. John do not tell me you plan on taking her truck again? Why not; it beats the hell out of walking all the way from here back to the Main Gate. Shit, besides that she is in the dorm kitchen with the other AH getting shit faced.

Thirty minutes later still in their SPC DIS John meets Susan at Maryrose's S-10 truck. Well Hon did you find anything worthwhile and exciting we may or can use? No nothing at all but a bunch of happy al-Qaida terrorist POS and NNGA POS getting shit faced in the dorm kitchen. I did not think you would. John I did not think Muslims drank alcohol! They don't except when they get caught, kind of reminds you of a bunch of Baptist Folks, HA! HA! Susan I am sure that most of the weapons they may have had stored around this place are now stowed on the "Elsa Cree". I did spot that old 1941 Packard Hearse you keep talking about, it's a beautiful old vehicle. Yes it sure is I saw it earlier when we walked in. I wonder what will ever become of it now that poor Adam Rasoul is no longer with us.

John and Susan get in the S-10 truck, John looks around no one in sight he starts the truck and slowly drives down the long lane towards the Main Front Gate. John what's in that big bag you put behind the back seat when you got in? Well my dear I did not count it but I am sure it's one million dollars in U.S.A. one hundred dollar bills, brand new a.k.a. Benny's. Susan laughs out loud and shouts "John you big AH you did not take Allen Rasoul's MC Christmas gift that the NNGA just gave him"? I sure did boy is he ever going to shit in his mess kit when he opens that MC present and finds that box empty. Did you rewrap it back up? I sure did just like I found it after I filled it up with a few old books, HA! HA! Merry Christmas my dear little Buttercup! John pulls up to the front gate it's locked as expected. He and Susan leave the S-10 parked and walk on up the road to their old Ford F-150 and return themselves back to a human state. They get in and drive on back up to the Delmarva Inn. On the way John looks over at Susan and says "well SPC Agent VA10C we had a good day and "did good" how do you like your SPC job"? Susan reply's, damn if it won't wear you out but it is exciting and as long as we can promote peace here on PE so be it, TYDL.

Back at the Delmarva Inn Susan and John decide to check out and not stay over, they also pass on supper, pack up the old Ford F-150 and decide to head home. Before checking out Susan makes reservations for December the 24th 25th and the 26th. Damn John I sure did not expect to be spending Christmas Eve and Christmas Day here on the Eastern Shore of Virginia. Me neither my dear! I am sorry but shit happens, we cannot take a chance on getting delayed in Christmas traffic and miss the "Elsa Cree" sailing away to Santiago Cuba. No worry John I realize that. Remember SPC Agent NV36C told us if any of those Prototype Exoset Missile Crates got hijacked it was our job to find it get it back or take it out. Remember also that he placed a SPC Sugar Cube in each "Driftwood Eagle" Crate for that reason. You ready dear, let's go home the Ole Piankatank River awaits us!!!!!

December 25, 2007 Tuesday. Allen, Maryrose, Dayzee and Dewey are all at Allen Rasoul's Cedar View farm to see their fellow al-Qaida Agents and other new NNGA German friends off and Bon Voyage on their cruise aboard the "Elsa Cree" to Santiago Cuba.

Dewey asks Allen how long do you expect them to be gone. Dewey I would estimate at least thirty days anyway by the time they transfer that Prototype Exoset Missile crate to the NNGA and go over all the details involved with Lt Ramey Sanchez. Nanki and Manki will pilot and return the "Elsa Cree" back here to the Farm. All the other agents have orders to remain on duty in Santiago Cuba with Rahism Badhdadi to support him and Lt Ramey Sanchez in the building up of the Cuban al-Qaida cell and hopefully oversee the NNGA development of the Exoset Missiles we so badly need to continue our cause. Dewey I am very excited about the way our future programs are developing and the future of our al-Qaida cause, Praise be to Allah!

It is now 1600Hr; everyone has been accounted for and have been onboard the Elsa Cree for hours taking care of final departure details. Nanki is on the bridge (Buddy Cree added to the top of the existing old Pilot House) and blows the boats horn to signal good bye. They all wave as the beautiful boat the "Elsa Cree" departs as they all sail away down through Nandua Creek on to the Chesapeake Bay then on to towards the Atlantic Ocean. Scheduled stops are planned for; at Charleston South Carolina, Savanah Georgia and the Florida Key's (Key Largo) for fuel, food and other supplies as necessary.

December 24, 2007 Christmas Eve Monday afternoon late. Susan and John arrive back at the Delmarva Inn from an uneventful drive over from their home on the Ole Piankatank River in Middlesex County. They check in unpack and go on to the Delmarva Inn Restaurant for a big Christmas Eve Seafood supper.

What will it be folks? Damn Tessie do you work all the time? Well I am single and unattached so I volunteered for the Christmas Holidays so the married folks can get off and be with their families. Damn that's mighty nice of you. Well they pay me double time plus the tips are great. Tessie bring us both the House Seafood Special and a big bottle of Merlot Wine. Coming right up folks!

John looks at Susan and says "hon perk up it's Christmas Eve". I know but it is the first time I can ever remember being away from home on Christmas Eve and Christmas Day and I am not Happy about it. I understand hon but by the time we complete our assigned SPC Missions over here just look at all the innocent lives we will save. John when you put it in that frame of mind it does make me feel a lot better, Peace on Earth good will towards Man, TYDL.

Well my dear it's getting late and if we don't get in bed before midnight "Old Saint Nick" may not come by, HA! HA! Susan let's just go back to our room, get a good night's sleep and rest. We have a big day coming tomorrow let's hope things go as planned.

December 25, 2007 Tuesday morning early. Both John and Susan are up early and well rested. Hon do you feel like having breakfast! Lord no not after that Seafood Supper we pigged out on late last night. Tessie said "she doubled up on a lot of our seafood items"! Well let's sit down and go over our plans once more and leave here about 1400Hr that will be time enough.

Hon it's about 1400Hr are you all set? Yes let's go! John and Susan leave the Delmarva Inn. John takes his time and drives straight down the Ole Delly Rode to the Southern Shore. He continues out and over the CBBT Steel Trestle Bridge on to Fisherman's Island. He gets to the nearest turnabout, pulls over and parks. He looks around no one insight. He and Susan go through their usual routine and put themselves in to their SPC DIS.

They stop and look around damn it is so beautiful out here. Are you cold? No my dear I wore this heavy jacket! Damn good thing its cool and blowing a fuckin gale, hell this wind will blow the hair off a dog's ass. Traffic is a lot heavier than I expected, but then again it's Christmas Day. Let's go as they walk back out, up and on to the CBBT Steel Trestle Bridge a. k. a. as the "High Rise". They get in position at the center span and just wait. Now what? Susan we just wait that's all we can do for now and hope for the best. If the "Elsa Cree" departed the Cedar View Farm on schedule she should pass under this High Rise about 1700Hr-1730Hr. My dear when that happens we let her pass under and sail clear of Smith Island then you; SPC Agent VA10C for the first time will have the honors to take her out and eliminate those five murdering al-Qaida POS onboard along with those two NNGA AH plus you will destroy the Prototype Exoset Missile crate as ordered by the SPCEBS. How about that; what a Christmas present, TYDL!

It is now 1705Hr as Susan and John strain their eyes looking out over the water finally they see the "Elsa Cree" sailing right towards them. Susan here she comes when she passes underneath let her continue sailing on towards the Atlantic Ocean and get almost out sight. When that takes place take your SPC CP and aim your invisible laser straight at the stern and transom area and lightly press your laser button. John you look sad! I am in away as I hate to see that beautiful restored old boat destroyed but shit happens.

They look down as the "Elsa Cree" passes underneath and continues on to the open Atlantic Ocean. As she begins to disappear from sight John tells Susan my dear zap her ass right in the transom. Susan a little nervous aims and presses the invisible laser button on her SPC CP. The explosion that follows is unbelievable the force is tremendous. John for heaven's sake I have never seen anything like that before in my life. John is also somewhat set back as he cannot believe that amount of force came from one small SPC Sugar Cube what a surprise. Susan still cannot believe her eyes as a huge white hot bubble engulfs the "Elsa Cree" as she vaporizes in 1200 Degree Fahrenheit super-heated steam. The steam burst through the top of the bubble everything is completely vaporized nothing but water droplets remain and begin to fall as the steam dissipates, nothing is left, nothing. A Huge Waterspout develops and raises high in to the clouds above.

Well my dear now you realize the power of your SPC Sugar Cubes and what they can do. Just think you eliminated five al-Qaida POS and two NNGA POS. All of them here and pledged to destroy our beautiful country and our way of life. Why! Why! Hon how do you feel now? John I feel wonderful, TYDL!

They put themselves back into a human state and drive back to the Delmarva Inn pull right up in front and park. John reaches over and gives Susan a big hug and a kiss. Hon you did a great job today JC and Lt Ree will certainly be satisfied that's for sure. By the way Merry Christmas and a Happy Birthday to our Dear Lord and Savior Jesus Christ, TYDL!

Back in their room John says lets freshen up go drink some Merlot Wine eat a big Seafood Supper and get shit faced. We can stay over and sleep in tomorrow and drive back home later. Sounds good to me! While we are at it let's stop by the front desk and confirm our reservation for tomorrow and make reservations for January the 01st Tuesday and January 02nd Wednesday 2008. Shit John I forgot we have unfinished SPC work at the WISC Complex. That's right my dear shit happens! At least we are promoting our SPC Peace Movement and saving innocent lives at the same time! John you are right, forgive me, TYDL

Chapter 26

WALLOPS ISLAND SPACE CENTER BOMB MISSION. SHUT DOWN AND TAKE OUT

January 01, 2008 Tuesday Happy New Years Day everyone. Again John and Susan drive back over from their Ole Piankatank River Home to the Delmarva Inn on the Eastern Shore. They check in unpack rest and discuss their SPC Shut Down and Take Out plans for tomorrow afternoon over at the WISC Complex.

John tells Susan let me handle things over at the WISC Complex tomorrow and you remain here and keep your eyes on the ARMA School House across the road. I have a big hunch Doc and his other thugs may show up over there to watch TV and celebrate their "So Call Big Bang" tomorrow right in his office.

January 02, 2008 Wednesday 1300Hr. John gives Susan a good bye kiss as he leaves to drive over to the WISC Complex. Hon, be careful and keep me informed on your SPC CP. I love you! I love you too! John leaves gets in his old Ford F-150 truck pulls out and heads on up the Ole Delly Rode North towards the WISC Complex. He arrives and drives into the WISC visitors parking area. He looks around and the coast is clear so he goes through his usual routine and puts himself in to his SPC DIS. He walks down through the WISC Complex Main Gate and on over to the Main Storage Warehouse. JC you AH this walking shit gets old after a while!!!!!!

As he walks in over on one side he sees a large area that has been set up as an Auditorium. He watches as food caterers are busy bring in and setting up big Food and Drink Bars. John thinks to himself this guy Charles Nutmaker knows how to do things up right. I heard he treats his employees very well and does an outstanding Management job running the WISC Complex.

John walks over and goes through the black curtains labeled "Bay 10" with the "Driftwood Eagle" sign attached. There they sit both of the "Driftwood Eagle" Crates. One containing the Prototype Exoset Missile Components from DAE and the other containing the al-Qaida High Yield Dynamite Round Stick Bomb that the al-Qaida Agent, Dewey Duzz constructed.

John stands and waits, he checks his watch it is now 1400Hr and the Warehouse is already packed with WISC personnel. Holy shit if that dynamite bomb was set off in here every one of these innocent folks would surely be killed or badly injured, God Help us. Can you believe those towel head bastards are this cruel! Why! Why! What in the hell is wrong with people! These POS have it made living over here in our beautiful U.S. A. and yet for some reason want to revert back to the fourth and fifth century conditions because a false God and a small book of some kind says so. Talk about sick bastards. Wake up people this is the twenty first century!

John walks over to the two "Driftwood Eagle" crates and stands beside the crate showing the "Driftwood Eagle" decals pasted on it upside down. He just stands and waits. SOB he cannot believe his eyes. This small well-dressed man walks up and stands behind the al-Qaida Dynamite Bomb Crate. Would you believe it is none other than Adam Rasoul's old friend and second in command from Topper's Field "Javid". John cannot believe Javid is the suicide (Martyrdom) bomber. Who would have guessed that? But what the hell John always thought Javid was a stupid PAS to start with and he did not like the SOB when he met him the first time over at Toppers Airfield in Hangar "A".

John watches as Javid connects his hand held transmitter to the detonation brass pins connecting the wooden oak handle to the crate. It is now 1420Hr. John steps over behind Javid, he reaches in his pocket and takes out a Hastings Beverage Company drink can. It is full of "Pigs

Blood". (His Last Can from the Nevada Edison Dam (NED) Mission in Las Vegas). He opens the can and pours it over Javid's head. He hands the empty can to Javid. Javid reads the label "Pigs Blood" and screams. As he screams John lightly touches Javid's neck. Javid collapses to the concrete floor dead from a SPC silent heart attack! It is now 1430Hr.

The chatter and conversation noise from the folks outside the black curtains overwhelm Javid's screams and no one comes to his aid. John looks down at the dead worthless PAS and thinks "I wonder what that AH did with mine and AL's old Piper J5 Airplane No. 40788"!

Meanwhile back at the Delmarva Inn Susan stands watch in Room No. 3 looking across the roadway at the ARMA School House. It is now 1200Hr. as Dr. Allen Rasoul and his mistress Maryrose drive up in his new Ford F-150 Club Cab Red Truck (thank you Buddy Cree for the new truck). They get out and walk inside to Allen's Office. A few minutes later Dayzee and Dewey drive up park and also walk inside.

All four of these POS sit in Allen's Office laughing, joking and celebrating the success of their two al-Qaida Delly Rode Cell Missions: The Hijacking of the Prototype Exoset (Driftwood Eagle Missile) Missile and the Primary Mission to bomb and destroy the WISC Complex. Susan puts herself in to her SPC DIS and decides it's time to walk over and see what's going on across the road and join the celebration she assumes is taking place. Susan gets there just as Doc turns on the TV Set.

A few minutes later Doc looks at the other three folks and say's "why in the hell are we all sitting here waiting and watching for breaking news reports about "Our Big Bang" on TV"! Hell let's ride up park and watch the real thing take place live. Damn Doc, great idea let's get going.

All four Doc, Maryrose. Dayzee and Dewey go out and get in Doc's new Ford F-150 and head on up Rt 13 towards Chincoteague. Susan still in her SPC DIS of course gets in the back and sits between Maryrose and Dayzee while Dewey sits up front with Doc. Doc drives on up Rt 13 and turns right on to Rt 175. As he drives Dayzee tells him to drive on down to the Second Turnabout and park it is has a larger spectator area and allows a better view of the WISC Complex. Doc follows her advice and pulls in to the Second Turnabout and parks! Dewey tells Doc this is a perfect viewing place as you can clearly see the WISC Complex in the far distance. Doc asks Dewey we are not to close; are we? Dewey laughs and says no Doc we are safe here but when that crated dynamite bomb goes off we will sure in hell know about it that's for damn sure. Dewy tells Maryrose and Dayzee to get their CPH cameras out and be ready as you sure do not want to miss this "Big Bang" it is going to be really special. "Praise Be to Allah"!

It is now 1415Hr. Doc again shouts "Praise Be to Allah" as all four POS sit and look towards the WISC Complex. Meanwhile Susan gets out of the truck stands close by and opens her SPC CP and removes a SPC Sugar Cube. She opens the gas fill flap door and places the SPC Sugar Cube just inside and quietly closes it. She walks down the road a safe distance from the truck stands and waits no hurry she has plenty of time.

January 02, 2008 Wednesday afternoon 1430Hr "Big Bang Time" has arrived. Doc again shouts "Praise Be to Allah"! Dead silence as they all continue to watch the WISC Complex area. Nothing, no explosion, nothing but silence "No Big Bang" what the hell is going on! The "Big Bang" should have taken place exactly at 1430Hr. All four sit in dead silence; watch, wait and listen then look at each other. They decide to wait as Javid may have been delayed and held up for some unknown reason who knows!

After waiting about an hour Doc opens his CPH and calls the WISC Complex Information Desk. Good afternoon WISC operator, how may I direct your call? Operator this is Dr. Allen Rasoul over at the ARMA, please direct my call over to one of your employees Mr. Javid the manager of the Main Storage Warehouse, Extension WH 804. Yes Sir, just a minute please!

Silence as the operator pauses! Operator are you still there? Yes Dr. Rasoul but I have some very sad news for you. Mr. Javid collapsed on the job early this afternoon. He was rushed to the General Hospital in Parksley and the staff there just reported back to us that he had passed on due to a massive heart attack. I am so sorry Dr. Rasoul was he a good friend of yours? No operator, not really just a nice guy and a long time business associate of mine, thank you operator have a nice day, good bye.

Dr. closes his CPH shakes his head as he looks at the other three al-Qaida agents and states "another failed mission". Our WISC inside agent Javid collapsed and died of natural causes before he was able to detonate the dynamite bomb crate. Allah please forgive us we have failed you once again.

Again Dr. looks over at the grim faces of the other three and say's "at least we can rejoice and take solace that one of our missions was a success; the Prototype Exoset Missile we hijacked is safely on its way to Santiago Cuba onboard the "Elsa Cree" as planned". (Little do they all know).

John puts his CP to his head and thinks VA10C. Susan answers and right away asks hon how did it go? Perfect my dear a piece a cake, no problems what so ever. Susan where are you? Would you believe just up the road from Chincoteague in a public spectator viewing area? People come here to watch WISC Complex Rocket Launchers and Lift Offs. Damn what in the world are you doing over there? The four al-Qaida POS; Doc, Maryrose, Dewey and Dayzee decided they would like to ride over here and witness their so called "Big Bang" take place live and in living color.

Where are they now? All four are sitting in Allen Rasoul's truck very dejected debating on what they need to do next. I have already placed a SPC Sugar Cube in the truck and was just getting ready to eliminate all four when you called. Hell hon do not let me interfere and stop you from completing these important proceeding. By all means go ahead and take them out now before they start to leave. OK let me do my thing and get it over with, just listen up. Susan switches her SPC CP over to the SPC Silent Invisible Laser program. She aims her SPC CP at the truck and depresses the invisible laser button. SOB what an explosion she can hardly believe her eyes as the entire truck is consumed and vaporizes that quick; nothing remains but a large crater in the Turnabout parking area. What a beautiful sight!

John did you hear that? Susan I sure did it was music to my ears. Four worthless murdering al-Qaida POS long gone that quick! John that Sugar Cube bubble engulfed that entire truck vaporizing it completely nothing left. John what a sight I wish you was here to have seen it, it was great.

Hon I am on my way to pick you up! Good I will be waiting and looking for you. Turn left on State Rt 175 I am at the Second Turnabout pull off. John arrives and picks up Susan as a small crowd begins to form. All eye witnesses that saw the explosion say it was a huge lightning strike and all they can see now is a small crater in the Turnabout parking area. As Susan gets in the truck she looks at John and says "Dear I know killing is a sin and I hope the Good Lord will forgive me but taking out those four POS sure makes me feel good".

As they drive back to the Delmarva Inn Susan say's to John "I know it's getting late but if it alright with you let's go back to the Delmarva Inn pack up, check out and get the hell out of Dodge and just go home. I know it is beautiful over here on the "Eastern Shore" but I have had enough and seen enough of the Delmarva Peninsula and the Eastern Shore of Virginia to last me for a fuckin life time that's for damn sure.

Chapter 27

CONCLUSION

January 11, 2008 Friday morning. John's CP vibrates, I be damn its Dennis Farrel SPC Agent NV36C calling from the SPCEBS. Hello Dennis! Good morning John how are you and Susan doing since you completed your latest two Missions over on the Delmarva Peninsula? We are doing very well, rested back to normal and we are not looking for anymore SPC work at this time! Do not worry I do not get involved with SPC Missions all of those assignments come through the SPCB on PA, JC and Lt Ree. I know Dennis, I was just kidding with you!

John the reason I called is that I am trying to close out my report so JC can review it and send it on to the SPCB on PA. The report speaks to your two "Delly Rode Cell" Missions. I have completed a rough draft I based on all the facts you sent us here at the SPCEBS. If you have time I would like to go over it and review it with you before I consider it complete and pass it on to JC. No problem Dennis I have plenty of time right now so let's start your review. Lt Ree told me he assigned this report to you and for Susan and me not to worry about filing it. Lt Ree told me to just send you a completed outline. Well John I am going to give you the facts and details I have; if you have any questions or changes just stop me and jump right in.

John to start with that young man the Aeronautical Engineer Cedric Fauntleroy "Nerdy" working with the DAE people is one clever and a very educated person. Dennis I know what you are saying Susan and I met him at the Delmarva Inn. DAE is fortunate to have him onboard.

Well John, Nerdy "Hoodwinked" all of us. What do you mean by that? How could he fool us? Well when our SPC people working inside of "Zone 52" gave him the heads up that an al-Qaida Cell working Stateside heard about his DAE Company getting ready to ship a completed Prototype Exoset Missile out for operational testing Nerdy's mind started to function. The first thing that came to his mind was "Hijacking". He needed to set up all DAE shipments to prevent any hijacking by any one. His next thought was in order for any outside activity to receive this kind of classified shipping information they would have to have inside support from an al-Qaida spy.

Nerdy as an experienced U.S. Army Intell man became suspicious of everyone working with or around him even his supervisor Norman Savage. Right off he noticed his new office assistant Anna Belle seems to be asking way too many questions about things she did not really have a need to know. She became his prime suspect and could be the al-Qaida inside spy who knows.

Unbeknown to Nerdy at this time he guessed correctly as we all now know. His new office assistant was Anna Belle and she was from Williamsburg Virginia. She was working undercover for a small suspected al-Qaida Cell working on the Delmarva Peninsula. Her boss and the Cell leader was Doctor Allen Rasoul and the Cell Code name is "The Delly Rode"!

John as an old retired law investigator you can appreciate how Nerdy hoodwinked us all: the SPCEBS, Zone 52, you, Susan, me and especially his suspected inside al-Qaida spy Anna Belle. He packed up two of the Prototype Exoset Missiles in to five Military Hypergolic Containers (MHC) (See Foot Note 3) each to be assembled on site by special MHC technicians. He then crated these ten MHC into two separate crates for shipment and gave them the Code Name "Driftwood Eagle". He had decals made showing the "Driftwood Eagle" code name design and pasted two decals on each of the two crates. To eliminate any terrorist group should they successfully hijack any of these crates he Booby-trapped each MHC with a small bomb he developed using a high yield dynamite round stick with a detonator cap and a flint friction pin attached to the MHC lid. Removal of this lid by anyone of course would detonate the bomb.

John, he then made arrangements to ship both of these crates to the WISC Complex in Wallops Island, Virginia. He also at the same time made travel plans for him and his assistant Anna Belle to follow later as consultants to support the WISC Complex Ordnance Technical people. This also was a diversion to support his plans.

John sit down for this! He then shipped two separate crates containing the actual Prototype Exoset Missile Components also packed in MHC code name "Driftwood Eagle" to the U.S. Eglin Air Force Base Test Facility located just outside of Valparaiso, Florida. SOB, Dennis you mean to tell me that the crate hijacked and stored onboard the Elsa Cree that sailed to Santiago Cuba contained nothing but five MHC each loaded with a homemade dynamite bomb? That's exactly correct my man a perfect Decoy set up by our DAE genius Nerdy himself.

Hell John Lt Ree and I were fooled to the point Lt Ree had already sent me over to the DAE Warehouse earlier to place a SPC Sugar Cube in each crate for the same reason Nerdy Booby-trapped them. When Susan's SPC CP silent laser beam from the High Rise Trestle struck the "Elsa Cree" and set off that SPC Sugar Cube plus Nerdy's added dynamite round sticks that is what caused such a larger than expected explosion to occur that surprised you so much. John at the present time Nerdy is not even aware of the fact one of his WISC crates was hijacked and exchanged and replaced with the al-Qaida crated dynamite bomb Dewey constructed. With this in mind I am sure JC is going to break with SPC PA tradition and send Nerdy a self-destructing modified CD copy of my finished report to update him in detail on exactly what took place.

John as bright as Nerdy is he did commit one serious mistake! Hard to believe; what was that? He left the Secret File Cabinet bar in his office off and unlocked one night. By doing this he allowed Anna Belle to have complete access to all of the Prototype Exoset Missile CPU Software. She of course made CD copies of all of this information, even the "Driftwood Eagle" decals. We now know she later passed all of this secret information on to Doctor Allen Rasoul at his ARMA School office.

John thank God you and Susan discovered those empty stolen Justin Conyers's High Yield Dynamite shipping boxes when you investigated Dewey's Junk yard Chop Shop. Also the fact that your law investigation experience allowed you to recognize a dynamite bomb had been constructed and assembled. John you and Susan, SPC Agents VA10A and VA10C saved the WISC Complex from total destruction and saved hundreds of innocent lives a long with it, TYDL, TYDL, TYDL!!!

Dennis what happens now to the two crates setting untouched up at the WISC Complex Main Warehouse? Well Nerdy in his last meeting with the WISC Director Mr. Charles Nutmaker went over and exposed his entire Prototype Exoset Missile Decoy plan and set up with him. Nerdy of course did not at the time nor does he know now that one of the crates would contain the al-Qaida Dynamite Bomb you defused no problem. John when Nerdy received confirmation from his Eglin Air Force POC that the two crated Prototype Exoset Missiles "Driftwood Eagle" he shipped to them had been received and were safe and secured he right away called Mr. Nutmaker at the WISC Complex. He told him any time after the Holidays to have his security people stand down and later have his ordnance people remove the "Driftwood Eagle" crates to a distant on site staging and strike down area and not to open them for any reason. At the staging and strike down area heavily spray and soak down each crate with kerosene oil and light them off. The crates including the MHC and dynamite will safely burn down to a small pile of ashes with no problems. John all of this we now know took place after you of course eliminated Javid.

Well John, VA10A all of this rough draft paraphrasing will be embellished and form my first Official report for the SPCEBS folks. What do you think and do you have questions or anything you would like to add? Yes Dennis I sure do! What the hell do I do with the one million dollars in Benny's I was able to obtain from Dr. Allen Raoul's home study at his Cedar View Farm? John I intentionally forgot to mention that money as it will not be in the Final Report. JC told me to tell "you and Susan just to keep it as a Christmas bonus for all your time, effort and a SPC job well done". What! Dennis we do not need this money and we are not greedy people by any means.

John what is your definition of "Greed". Dennis my definition of greed is: "The Sadists Desire to have more of what you already have but do not really need"! Dennis Greed is the root to all things that are EVIL!!!!! Wonderful, I agree 100% with you John. John just give the damn money away to your Middlesex County, Virginia Volunteer Organizations incognito they can all use it I am sure of that. Dennis great idea consider it a done deal.

Well John that's about it, that's all I have! Dennis it is an excellent report and gets my full approval! Thank you John! Dennis tell that beautiful Desiree hello and keep us posted on the big wedding date Susan and I will certainly be there with bells on. Keep in touch good bye! Will do, good bye John!

John what do you think? Bout what! Damn John look over here at my new "Driftwood Eagle" framed decal pictures. Susan they are beautiful pictures. Thank you, I went ahead and framed all four of the "Driftwood Eagle" decals. Susan the wood carving in the decal picture is beautiful, who carved it? On the back side of the decal it reads "Another Carving Masterpiece by John Jones". Damn Susan we have several of his original hand carved birds we purchased from him in person at the Virginia Living Museum Wildlife Festival in Newport News, Virginia a few years ago. Great, he does excellent work.

John look at this it was in the envelope with the Driftwood Eagle decals. What is it? It's a sealed crystal with a Compact Disc (CD) inside. It's not the latest "Firefall Album is it? No, not hardly Garlee said "they are still working on that in the studio." The outside label reads "Yellow Cake WHS1945 CD (2) give to Dayzee." Hell it is probably just a Pound Cake recipe that belongs to Dewey's wife Dayzee that got put in there by accident. Maybe I will just keep it awhile and put it up in the kitchen cabinet with my other recipes and cook books.

John I think I will hang one Driftwood Eagle picture in the den and one in the Boat House patio. I plan on giving one to Linda and one to Helen. Wonderful just make sure you have a good story line made up when they ask you as usual where you got them beautiful decals. Hon, remember no connection ever relating to the SPC. Hell John you AH, I know the SPC Code and Routine: its collect your "Atta boys" drop your draws and bend over it's all settled but the color of the Vaseline. John laughs, my dear spoken like a True Blue VA10C SPC Agent. Hell, Hon its past 1200Hr let's go get a cold beer and hang your two new "Driftwood Eagle" decal pictures.

To Be Continued!!!!!!!!!!

Foot Notes

1. Front Cover Picture. This picture is a Photograph of a full size American Bald Eagle Head carved from Bass Wood and mounted on a piece of Red Oak Driftwood. It was hand carved and developed by the Books Author John Jones in February 1999.

2. Money Cubes (MC) are exactly that. A heavy cubed shaped box that is sized to hold one million dollars in one hundred dollar U.S. Treasury Bills a.k.a. Benny's. One MC weighs twenty two pounds, (ten kilograms). Most Criminal Groups and Terrorist Groups trade in U.S. Currency. When trading in large sums they use and weigh out MC in lieu of (time consuming) counting individual bills. Note: Believe it or not there is some trust even among thieves.

3. Military Hypergolic Containers (MHC). These are Specially Designed Containers used to ship and / or store Special Weapons or weapon components that require a controlled atmospheric condition until it's time to assemble and / or ready the weapon involved for use.

Glossary

ACSD	Accomac County Sheriff's Department.
AEA	Albert Edward Aerodrome.
AH	Ass Hole.
a.k.a.	Also known as.
APB	All-Points Bulletin.
ARMA	Allen Rasoul Marine Academy.
ASAP	As soon as possible.
AT	Air Tram.
Beam	Maximum width of a boat.
Benny's	Slang for a U.S.A. 100 dollar Treasury bill. (Benjamin Franklin's picture on the bill).
BS	Bull Shit.
BSD	Bachelor of Science Degree.
CAD	Computer Aided Design.
CBBT	Chesapeake Bay Bridge Tunnel System.
CD	Compact Disc.
Chop	Slang for stripping a vehicle down in to usable separate parts.
CP	Cell Pad (SPC Weapon).
CPU	Computer Processing Unit.

CPH	Cell Phone.
3-DI	Three Dimension Images CAD.
DAE	Dekamp Aviation Engineering Company.
Detail	This means to completely wash, clean and polish a motor vehicle in its entirety from top to bottom.
DIS	Demineralize Invisible State (SPC Weapon).
DMV	Division of Motor Vehicles Department.
Dr.	Doctor.
Draft	The depth of a boats hull below the waterline.
e.g.	For example.
EM	Electronic Computer processed Mail.
Hr	Hundred Hours.
Intell	U.S. Army Intelligence Office & research Headquarters.
etc	et-cetera.
FBI	Federal Bureau of Investigation.
ISBN	International Standard Book Number.
JC	Joshua Christian. SPCEBS Commanding Officer.
K	One thousand.
Lt	Lieutenant.
LOA	Full length of a boat over all.
MC	Money Cube. (see Foot Note 2).
MCSD	Middlesex County Sheriff's Department.
MD	Mickey Dees. (Fast food restaurant).
MHC	Military Hypergolic Container. (See Foot Note 3).
mm	Millimeter.
NED	Nevada Edison Dam, a.k.a. Nedy.
No.	Number.
NNGA	Neo-Nazi German Army.
PA	Planet Ares.
PAS	Piece a Shit.
PDQ	Pretty Damn Quick.
PE	Planet Earth.
PHD	Philosophy of Doctors Degree.
POC	Point of Contact.
POS	Piece of Shit.

Rt	Route.
SC	Sugar Cube (SPC Weapon).
Sgt	Sargent.
SPC	Secret Peace Corp.
SPCB	Secret Peace Corp Board. (located on PA).
SPCEBS	Secret Peace Corp Earth Base Station.
SOB	Son of a Bitch.
SRR	Squadron Ready Room.
TDY	Temporary Duty.
Triple "S"	Military slang for Shit, Shower and Shave.
TV	Television Set.
TYDL	Thank You Dear Lord.
U.S.A.	United States of America.
VASP	Virginia State Police.
VIN	Vehicle Identification Number.
WDR	Wood Duck Ridge.
WHS	Warwick High School
WISC	Wallops Island Space Center.
XPDJP	Experimental Drone Jet Propulsion.

About The Author

John was born and raised in Newport News Virginia. He graduated from Warwick High School and later from William & Mary VPI Extension (Now Old Dominion University), Norfolk, Virginia. He retired after 42 years as a Marine Design Engineer.

John is married to the best little gal in the World and they live in Middlesex County, Virginia on the Ole Piankatank River. TYDL.

CPSIA information can be obtained
at www.ICGtesting.com
Printed in the USA
BVHW031045070219
539718BV00004B/41/P